A

A Time To Weep

Lollie

Copyright © 2012 Lollie

ISBN:1499781245

ISBN-13:9781499781243

The New Partner

"This latch activates the signal within a continental distance." Fred pointed to a tiny hook where the shoestring threaded. He was showing Nicholas how to use the tracking device for the next assignment. "Just simply kick it against something hard to begin the tracking."

"How do I deactivate it in case I accident … a … lee …" Nicholas trailed off in distraction.

Fred looked to see what was so important that this new guy couldn't pay attention to this very important demonstration. Following Nicholas's gaze, his lips spread into a wide grin.

"That is one of our top-level security agents. She's top-notch, both on and off the job." He watched the awed expression and goaded the new agent even more with a twinkle in his eye. "Refreshing as a bright summer day isn't she? Beautiful, charming, smart, oh and married."

Nicholas immediately turned back to the shoes in question, feeling slightly ashamed. The vision that passed before him was possibly the most beautiful thing God could have made. The most charming body filled a simple black dress complimented by a strand of pearls and dainty black and white shoes. The brim of a lovely matching hat concealed her face, until she turned to smile at Zeke, the computer expert agent. It was at that point that Nicholas caught a glimpse of her majesty.

She had smooth natural skin and a smile that could charm honey from bees. He couldn't see any flaws from a distance. If he could ... then Fred's voice filtered through his thoughts, "married." He should have looked for a wedding band first thing. Of course, she would be married, and he had looked upon her in admiration.

At the conclusion of his training, Nicholas went to the gym to work through some of the guilt he was feeling. The more he thought about the married woman, the harder and faster he thrust the hydraulic weights over his head. Why was a total stranger having this effect on him?

Amidst these thoughts, his superior interrupted, "Park, have you met our newest team member, Nicholas O'Ryan?"

"Mr. O'Ryan, I have heard so much about you. It is very nice to put a face with the name." There *she* stood with her hand outstretched to him, and a smile that melted his heart. "Your reputation precedes you."

Nicholas hesitantly reached out a sweaty hand to meet hers with a quickening heartbeat. Suddenly he felt even hotter than he had a minute ago. He reddened in humble embarrassment. "Oh, don't believe everything you hear."

"How long have you been in our division, Mr. O'Ryan?" There was no way of avoiding her eyes, for they searched clearly for his. Surely, she was reading his thoughts with the bluest eyes he had ever seen.

"Three weeks. How about you?"

"Oh, I have been here forever, or so it seems."
Her laugh was a sweet melody.

"Yes, Stevens has been our top agent until you
arrived, O'Ryan. I am excited to see what the two of
you can accomplish together." Mr. Richardson led
her away.

Richardson tried out his theory as he coupled the
two top agents on the next assignment. Nicholas
found Park Stevens to be quick, efficient, and self-
reliant. The two complimented each other without
much verbalization. Both excelled in what they did
and the two minds came together as one, for the most
part. Richardson was right. Together they were a
dynamite team.

They returned from their first assignment, which
lasted four days, when Park made an offer Nicholas
could not refuse. "I want you to come over tonight
for dinner, if you can. My husband wants to meet my
new partner. You can bring someone."

Nicholas agreed heartily. "After everything you
have told me of your husband, I would like to meet

this one-of-a-kind man. What time, and what should I bring?"

"Just bring your appetite. How does five o'clock sound?"

"I'll be there."

He looked at the address she handed him on a paper as if it were a foreign language, because he didn't know where anything was in this town. He questioned the only person he knew to ask, and Fred agreed to show him the way.

Fred was older, but he was a kid at heart. He enjoyed playing the part of the jokester, but when it came to Park, he became protector. He made it his responsibility to observe her new partner to make sure he was of the right stuff. His initial impression was that he liked Nicholas, but could one always tell a person by first impressions? He better be the best partner his Precious could have. "Precious" was Fred's pet name for Park. Park was the daughter he never had.

Welcome

Park had called her husband before inviting everyone over for dinner, and there was nothing in the world more thrilling to Matthew Stevens than putting a smile on his wife's face. They had been apart for four long days while she was on this assignment, not to mention the task that kept her away for two-weeks prior, so he left work after her phone call, picked up their daughter from the sitter, and arrived home at the same time as his wife.

He greeted her with his usual kiss, "Welcome home, Honey. We sure missed you."

"Oh, Matt, I am so glad to be home, and there is my Sarah girl." She gathered her nineteen-month-old in her arms. "I hate these long assignments, I feel like I am missing her grow up."

"And is that all you miss?" Matt teased in mock hurt.

She wrapped her arm around his waist, "Of course

not, I miss Spirit too." her laugh was music to his ears.

"Oh, you missed your horse more than me. Uh-huh, I see how it is." He sniffed for pitying effect. "Well, maybe I should go sleep in the barn tonight, where I'll be welcome." He pulled away from his wife with an indignant look.

Park reached for him again with a welcome kiss, "Okay, but I am not mucking your stall."

As Matt helped his wife prepare for their company, she watched his back. He was such a fine man. He was strong and extremely handsome. His Air Force uniform made his charm irresistible. His blond hair shining in the sunlight made a crowning effect. However, his physique was not what made Park fall in love with him. He had overcome so many hardships to become a wonderful, loving, and incredible person. She felt very blessed. God had given her a perfect husband, a perfect daughter, and one more on the way.

The couple's oldest and dearest friend was the first

to arrive at the party. Bruce and Park grew up together in the same small town. He had eight sisters, but none of them was as close as he and Park. They were always considered the daring duo.

Park introduced Matthew to Bruce in high school, turning the daring duo into the terrific trio of best friends. All three joined the Air Force, sealing their friendship for life. There were several years of separation, but they managed to be reunited.

During his stay overseas, Bruce fell in love with and married a beautiful young woman. Claire never had the opportunity to meet her husband's best friends, because of an auto accident that took her life, shortly after giving birth to their daughter, Sonya. This misfortune relocated him to the United States.

Sonya would always be the apple of her daddy's eye, but lately, he had taken another interest. He had been dating the gorgeous fair-haired Christy for several months. Sonya had no problems sharing her daddy with Christy, as she loved her also.

Matt and Park greeted the remainder of guests as a

part of the family as well. Nicholas couldn't help admiring and liking his partner's husband. He was a strong character and held himself confident. He exhibited the same characteristics that Nicholas found appealing in Park.

In turn, Matt liked Nicholas. He was a Christian, and Matt was comfortable in knowing this man would see to his wife's safety. He knew she could take care of herself, but as is with any sacred thing, he wanted to ensure her coming home at the end of the day, especially now that she was expecting his second child.

The Stevens' house looked upon the beautiful Atlantic Ocean. As the dinner party moved outside, the brilliant colored sunset brought forth private exclamations of delight, displaying God's magnificence in its truest form.

Late in the evening, the guests drifted off until the three were alone again. Park made haste in cleaning up, while Matt bathed Sarah and prepared for bed.

"Honey," whispered Matt to his lover after they

had gone to bed, "Ten years ago, did you ever think we would be this gloriously happy?"

"Mmmmm," his wife sleepily replied nestling closer. She felt comfort in her husband's heartbeat under her ear. She never felt such a sense of belonging and love. She had no problem falling quickly into a dream sleep.

New Adventures

The next four months passed slowly for Park. They repeatedly proved Richardson's theory by being a complimentary unit. Both had brilliant minds and shared similar opinions. In the heat of battle, one would react before the other had to speak a word of instruction.

The only drawback to his energetic team was that after the first three months, Richardson had to separate them, because Park was beginning to show in her pregnancy.

He coupled Park with Zoë, a wizard at the computer, who taught her a few tricks of the trade. Much to her aggravation, Richardson chained her to the office, until after the baby was born. She hated not being in the middle of the action.

Because of her disdain for holding down the fort, Matt thought it best to wait until the last possible moment before disclosing his news to her. He dreaded.

It was during the party for Sarah and Sonya, who had begged their parents to throw a joint birthday celebration, because they were determined to be sisters one way or another, that Matt decided it was now or never. He had to tell her tonight.

It was in the midst of the gaiety that he quietly explained he had to go overseas for two weeks. Park said little. She dreaded the sound of this very much. It was different, when she was gone for her job, but she was about to find out how hard this was on Matt.

She was not looking forward to his being gone. How would she get along without him? What if he didn't make it back in time for the birth? She would not; she absolutely refused to have this child without him there! She would go and talk to General Kincaid. She would put it in simple terms. "Let my husband stay home!"

Park knew that it was top secret and dared not ask any questions about it, no matter how much it drove her crazy. She knew in her heart that this was his job, his duty, and she could not be selfish. He would go for his country and serve it honorably. She was proud of him for his bravery and accomplishments; yes, even if it meant a solo childbirth.

"I'll be overseas for two weeks, and I don't want you to sit here and get yourself worked up about it. You go out on these assignments and come back safe and sound all the time, so wipe that frown off your pretty face." He was consoling the night before he was to leave. He could see his absence was going to be hard on his pregnant wife. "I'll put Sarah to bed and be in after you take your shower."

He carried Sarah upstairs to her room with extra slow steps. "How does Park do this all the time?" he thought. He was only going away one time, and it was killing him. He lingered with his daughter, until he heard the water in shower down the hall stop running.

"Now Sarah, I'll be leaving for a couple of weeks real early in the morning. You be a big girl and help Mommy out. She will need you to be on best behavior until your little brother or sister is born? Can you do that for Daddy?"

Her golden curls tossed as she shook her head affirmatively, "You doe way wike Mommy?"

"That's right honey. Just like Mommy. Some day you will understand why Mommy leaves us for work. Her job is important for stopping the bad people in the world."

"You dob portint?"

"Yes it is very important. Now, you get some sleep, and when I come back, we'll get your little brother or sister and go get ice cream."

"Will my bwudda or tista wike ice tweme? I div it chwockit," she accepted her Dad's kiss and then lay down contented.

"Goodnight, my angel." Her soft fresh baby scent left a memory in his heart, as he knelt in observance, until the tiny lashes lay on baby cheeks.

"Park, have you thought of a name yet?" Matt asked distractedly coming out of the shower, "What if it is a boy?"

Park smiled, "His name will be Matthew, just like his Daddy."

He pounced onto the bed throwing his wet head in her lap and laughed. "What if it is a girl?"

She pushed him away quickly and wiped the water from her arms, "I haven't thought much about it. Did you have something in mind?"

"We could name her after you," he suggested.

"I do not think so Matt. We would never know which Park you were talking to."

"I wasn't talking about Park, I was thinking of Ma..."

"No!" interrupted Park, "That is forgotten, you promised me. Matt, you cannot bring that..."

"I'm sorry. It was just a thought. Anyway, I will be back before the little one is born to name it myself. I didn't mean to upset you." He pulled into his arms. "You are so very dear to me. I would rather cut my tongue out than to say anything to cause you pain."

Park kissed his hand. "I know."

"I'll miss you more than you'll ever know." He returned a kiss to her hand. "When you're out on assignment, this bed gets so lonely." He pulled her face to look into her eyes. "When I get back, we both need to look into getting a job that will keep us closer to home."

"Honey, there are reasons why we do what we do," Park interjected.

"Responsibility begins at home. What does it profit us to gain the whole world, if we lose our own home? We are going to have another little one. I just don't want to miss one minute of his or her life. I have missed so much of Sarah's. I have had a lot of time to think about this. This assignment really has me reconsidering staying in the military."

"Everything will be alright, Honey. Once you get back, we can make all the changes in the world."

"Promise me you won't find some handsome fellow to take your mind off your loneliness, while I am gone."

Park exposed her pregnant belly from beneath the

blanket. "Right; some man would look at a beached whale. If anybody does any looking, it will be you."

"Park, you know you are the only woman for this old bum." He kissed her hair. "You will miss me when I am gone, won't you?"

"I miss you already, Mr. Stevens."

"I love you."

Park whispered, "I think I have loved you forever." She ventured off on a memory, "I didn't think you would ever love me. You would not look at me twice."

"You were a scraggly tomboy, not to mention my best friend. Then, you used your womanly wiles on me. Bruce nagged to get me to look at you as more than a kid." He pulled her tighter, "Remind me to thank him."

"Me too," Park murmured into his neck.

"Three o'clock is too early for you to get up, my love, and my son needs his rest, so you just stay in bed in the morning. I can see myself off." Matt patted her stomach.

"Mmmm," Park mumbled, already half-asleep.

Goodbyes

Matt's leaving coincided with Park's first day of forced leave of absence. Contrary to his orders, she rose early in order to spend as much time as she could with her betrothed.

They lingered over their good-byes, until Matt was in danger of being late, and then Park tried to figure out what she was supposed to do all day.

After seeing Sarah off to preschool, she spent her morning cleaning the house, lunging her sleek black thoroughbred, and cleaning him and his stall.

For lunch, she joined Fred at the Magnolia gardens, where they had an hour of wonderful fellowship. Park escorted him back to work, where Nicholas greeted them with a smile, "Well, Partner, looks like you are still out of the game for a while. Are you ever going to have that baby and come back to work?"

Park laughed, "Soon. Looks as if I don't hurry

back, though, I can be replaced."

"No one could ever replace you, Mrs. Stevens." A young woman standing beside Nicholas declared.

Nicholas shaded red in awkwardness. "Excuse my manners. Park, this is Jenny, my temporary partner. Jenny, you know Fred, and this is Park."

Park reached out to shake the extended hand. "It is a pleasure to meet you. Jenny, are you a full-level officer?"

"Not quite. I still have a few weeks in training. Nicholas is a wonderful teacher. I stand by my statement," her voice was sweet and youthful. "You are irreplaceable."

Park smiled modestly, when a light came to her eyes. "Listen, my husband will be returning in two weeks. Let's plan a get-together for a homecoming celebration. Jenny, Nicholas knows where we live. You could come with him. Would you all come?" She waited for the affirmative nods.

Fred laughed nodding at her stomach, "Are you going to throw this shindig at the hospital?"

Park smiled at his jest, "Hardly. I still have a while to go."

"If you say so. You look as if you're gonna pop any minute now," he shook his head, enjoying the laugh he received from his cohorts.

She patted her belly dramatically, "If you think that is bad, you should be in my shoes. I can't even see my shoes." She placed a kiss on the old wrinkled cheek. "I'll call you as soon as I find out the specifics of his arrival time."

"Sounds like a plan."

"Well, I guess I better let you get back to work. Thanks for lunch. See you soon, I hope." Nicholas and Jenny continued on their way. Turning to Fred, Park added, "You know, you need not wait for an invitation to come over to our house. The door is always open." With a smile and another peck on the cheek, she left the old friend gleeful as a child.

However, two weeks felt like two months. The idle time left Park very bored, and that gave her the sensation that time was standing still. Even the time she spent shopping for Sarah and Sonya, riding, and the countless hours she spent teaching them to ride did little to speed up time.

The two weeks turned into a third, and there was no word from Matt. A worried Park contacted General Kincaid since Bruce was gone on some military expedition. Although she knew he would be unable to answer top-secret questions, she must try to find any bit of information. As a result to her query, his only reply was a hint that Matt was due back on Thursday.

It was not enough to settle her worry, but it gave her something to do to occupy her angst. She called up Fred and made plans for a welcome home party for Matt. She decided to throw it on Thursday, because if she went to all the trouble to throw this party, surely he would come home that day.

She forced out any thoughts that he might miss the due date. She refused to think that he would risk missing the birth of their child by cutting his return so close. The thought of no husband or best friend to be there at the birth of her child caused Park to feel alone for the first time in quite a few years.

Tuesday passed, and then Wednesday. She could hardly keep her mind on the prayer meeting, thinking of her lover's return on the morrow. Her thoughts teetered between Elisha's walk with God and the memory of Matt's sweet smile.

On Thursday, Fred arrived first to help Park hang the "Welcome Home" banner. She showed him the cake decorated in Air Force emblem, and the punch she had prepared, but Fred could see she was deeply concerned. Though she tried to cover, there was nervousness in her voice and a small quiver in her hand.

Over the next hour, other guests drifted into the cozy home, including a few friends of Matt's from the base, yet, there was no guest of honor. Some began to swim in the ocean, while others frolicked on the beach. Nicholas volunteered to manage the barbeque pit, until the host arrived. Jolly sounds and incredible aromas began filling the air. Yet, where was Matt?

Park, watchful of the door, was the first to spot Bruce coming through the kitchen. "My goodness, where have you been?" Park cheerfully asked when she saw a grim expression on his face. Christy was not with him, which made her think there was trouble between the two. She put a false lilt in her voice and avoided mentioning Christy.

"What's all this?" he asked waving his arm around.

"Why, it is party for my husband. I figured he could not refuse coming home, if I wanted it bad enough."

"I wish you hadn't done this." He fumbled with his Air Force hat edgily.

"Where is my husband? Why are you alone?" She looked questioningly over his shoulder, feeling something awry. She knew it went beyond Bruce's girlfriend. "Where is Christy? I told her to bring you and Matt."

"Listen, I need to talk to you," looking at Fred he

added, "alone."

Fred kissed her cheek and stepped away from the area of the deck, "I'll be close, if you need anything."

Bruce continued mechanically. This was very hard, but it had to come from him. "Park, I've been on a rescue mission to liberate Matt and his men after they were captured."

Park held her breath in disbelief. "How can that be? Matt is the best they have. He does not get caught." Bruce continued to hold his head low in silence. Park hoped, even though she felt the truth in her soul, "Is he at the hospital? Is he hurt badly? Take me to him. Come on," she pleaded with eyes and voice, but still received no response. "What is it Bruce? What are you not telling me?"

"I can't take you to him, Park. I failed you and him. We reached him too late. His men told me they killed him two days before we arrived."

Park was not listening anymore. She grabbed her reeling head as if in attempt to stop it before it beat her to death. Matt was dead, that is all she heard...

her beloved Matt. He would not be coming back as he promised. It resounded echoing through her seemingly hollow skull. Killed…killed…KILLED!

The Party Is Over

The following minutes were a blur to Park Stevens. Bruce noticed her ashen face and trembling legs. Fearful, lest she would fall, he put his arm around her back, gently directing her to a deck chair, and then he went and brought her some water.

After a moment, Bruce guided her to the den, "That heat is too much. This is better. Park, are you okay?"

"How do you know he is dead, Bruce? How do you know they didn't just torture him and move him to another site? Did you see him at all? Maybe they took him to another location. I'll go myself and find him. Who was with him? I need to talk to them. They can tell me where he is." She was rambling to herself mostly.

"He went in with Simmons and Barrett. They were all three tortured severely. Barrett told me that they separated Matt Saturday, and that he died on

Monday." He did not want to divulge how that torture was the method of death. He could never let her know the torment Matt suffered. "They can tell you more, but in the end, Matt is still gone." He couldn't bring himself to say the word 'dead'. "They are at the base hospital. Do you want me to take you there?"

"No, I won't intrude on them while they are recuperating. I will wait until they are released."

"I'm sure they would understand. They know how Matt loved you. They would want you to know what happened."

"Bruce, will you see to my guests? I need some air."

"Of course, do you want me to find Sarah for you?"

"No, would you watch her for me tonight? I need to find a way to tell her that Daddy's not coming home....," she gasped on the, "ever."

"Sure Sweetie, go ahead. She'll be fine with us. Take all the time you need."

Park didn't wait to change her clothes or grab her purse. Ignoring the pains shooting through her stomach, she ran to her Jeep and left, thinking only about Bruce's words. Her reason for living was gone. God, You know he was my world.

Bruce went back to the throng of people with the heaviness of loss in his heart. He lost his best friend in the whole world, save the one who just walked out of the door, yet he had to greet all those friends that were here to celebrate the homecoming of one who would not be coming home. He regretted telling Park he would do this, but there was no one else to do it.

Fred was on the alert ever since he saw Park turn deathly white. He didn't know what Bruce told her, but he knew it was not good. He waited anxiously for Precious to return. When Bruce came out, he quickly grabbed him.

"Is Park in labor? She looked awful sick?"

"No sir, she just had a dose of bad news," replied Bruce.

"Don't tell me the good-for-nothing bum isn't

coming home tonight." he tried to lighten the mood. The look that came over Bruce's face made him recant his lightheartedness.

"That 'good-for-nothing bum' is never coming home." Bruce's good nature failed him in light of the somberness. He had taken offense to Fred's folly.

Realizing what Bruce had just told him, Fred wanted to fall into a hole and disappear. The facts had dawned upon him too late, and his joke was grossly out of place. "What happened?"

"I would rather you hear any more from Park." Bruce's tone announced that his opinion of Fred was irreparably damaged.

"Sure, look, I'm sorry for what I said."

"Me too." Bruce waved his apology away.

"I know that Matt is anything but a good-for-nothing. I greatly respected the man. He was a good father and wonderful husband. I know Park thought the world of him. Where is Park? Is she all right?"

Bruce was reluctant to disclose any information. "She needs time."

"Sure. Do you want me to help you get rid of some of the guests? O'Ryan and Silvers came with me."

"Much obliged to you sir."

Fred quietly pulled the two friends from work aside and told them it was time to leave, but didn't reveal the reason for their hasty retreat until the ride home. A pall veiled the trip home.

It fell to Bruce's lot to find a way to get the rest of the guests to leave without questioning the reasons. He did this in short order by explaining an emergency had come up causing the hostess to take leave.

After all were gone, he gathered Sarah in his arms to take her home with him, with a brief comment that she was going to spend the night with Sonya. Oblivious to the circumstances, the girl was gleeful at the news. It was so hard to see Matt's little girl so happy, when he knew Matt would never lay eyes on her again.

The Aftermath

Park couldn't breathe. She wanted her world to fold up and go Home. She no longer desired to exist. How would she tell Sarah? How could she raise two children alone? Then, she remembered in her misery that Matt would never see his second child. He would not be there for its birth. He had promised, and now he could not keep that promise.

She found herself at the stable a couple of miles from her home. She didn't bother to saddle Spirit; she just bridled and with some difficulty, mounted the wide haunches of the magnificent beast in a sidesaddle fashion.

Spirit was one of the first things Matt bought his new bride, because he knew how much she loved riding. Park broke the young Thoroughbred and trained him to respond to a mere pressure point or whistle. He sensed the delicate creature riding upon his broad back, and with gentility, he gaited along the beach. The sun was setting another beautiful scene, but Park was unaware of it.

Park was not one to give in to tears, but she couldn't stop them now. She wiped them away, but they just kept coming. They were beyond her control.

The rays began sinking behind the faraway ridges. The wind coming off the ocean blew Park's white dress into ripples around her. The pins began releasing her hair, as the curls played around her face. A man sitting on a motorcycle in a little hide-away cove watched as she passed by at a distance with the thought, "She is an angel God sent down to earth."

What wee hours of the morning Park returned home, she did not know. Her life seemed to be an 'out of body' dream, and she could not make anything feel alive. The house was so cold and empty. It almost had a malicious taunt in the night shadows. Sitting in Matt's chair, the tears welled up, once again, and then overflowed. There was a faint smell of his cologne lingering on the fabric. Every detail in this house screamed Matt's name, leaving a painful memory. Park couldn't handle it anymore. She had to get out of this house.

She must prepare for telling Sarah. It was good that she was with Sonya. "Oh God," she breathed, "help me I pray in the name of my Heavenly Father."

Again, she climbed into her Jeep. It was time for her to face the situation and tell Sarah. She prayed the whole way, for grace. What words could she say to a two year old? How? Why? "Oh Matt!" she cried out while waiting for a traffic light to change green. "Why did you leave us? We need you so much."

Sonya responded to her knock. "Hi, Aunt Pawuk"

"Hi Kitten, are you two girls having fun?"

"Uh-Huh, Sawah gibbed me hurwuh dollie. It was the pwettiest one she had. Daddy says I dot to gibbed hurwuh sompin back."

"Oh no, Sweetheart, you keep that doll, and you keep your toys, too. Sarah has plenty. She enjoys sharing with you. You are the best little friend she has. Best friends are very important."

"Mommy! Mommy!" Sarah saw her mother and ran to her with open arms. "Did Daddy det home?" She looked up at her mother with hope in her eyes.

Once again, she ignored the shooting pains in her abdomen. Park looked over at Bruce pleadingly, "Not tonight, Honey."

They finished breakfast and their morning devotions, when Bruce called the children into the living room for 'the talk'.

They bowed their heads as Bruce led them to the Throne of Grace. "Dear Heavenly Father, hear our prayer this day. Please forgive us our sins, for they are many. Please shed your cleansing blood upon our wretched wicked souls. Please help us with the task before us. Please comfort these that only You can comfort. Heal the wounds, I pray. In the precious name of Jesus we pray, and for His sake we ask these things, Amen." The burden seemed to have been lighter after having asked for His help.

"Sarah," Park began, "we found out yesterday that

Daddy will not be coming to our home any more."

"Did he pined nudder home?" Sarah's eyes filled with curiosity.

"Well, in a way. You see... It is like this...."

Bruce came to the rescue, "Do you remember just now, when we prayed Sarah?"

"Uh-Huh"

"Well, who did we pray to?"

"I knowed, Daddy!" interjected Sonya getting into the game. "Yoouh Hebenwy Fodda."

"That is right, Sweetheart. Now, where does our Heavenly Father live?"

"In Heben," Sonya was bouncing on the couch clapping her hands, thinking it was a game. Park couldn't help the smile that crossed her lips as she watched these two young innocent souls exploring God. They should never have to face this kind of agony. Maybe they would not feel the ramifications so strongly being barely two years old.

Bruce continued, "When it is our appointed time, we will go to be with Him and live in Heaven, but only if you are saved by the blood of Jesus Christ."

"My Daddy is sabed," this from Sarah.

"Yes, he was," Park finally brought sound to her voice. "He was a wonderful man, and I know he went to Heaven, because he *was* saved. That is his new home."

"Did he det tireded ob us?"

Park wrapped her child as closely as she could, "Oh, No! He loved us very much, but it was his appointment to go. Jesus needed him more than we did. Daddy had a hard life and now it is time for him to rest."

"Den I don't wike Desus. He taked my Daddy." The brows of this child knit perplexedly.

"Sarah, don't blame God. Did you know that His Son, Jesus Christ, King of Heaven and earth, came down from His throne to live with a sinful people? He was perfect and never did anything wrong. You know how sometimes you would tell Daddy that you were scared just so he would come and give you extra kisses?" After an affirmative nod she continued, "That is sin, and that is wrong. Jesus never did anything wrong at all. God sent Him to live on this earth so He could die for you and me and Daddy. Now, if He gave His Son who knew no sin, should we not give Daddy who did sin? He is where he can never see sin ever again. And someday, when it is our appointed time, we will be with Daddy in his new home."

"I wanna doe, now."

"Me too!" shouted Sonya.

"You will go if you are saved." Park sighed. How could Sarah be so happy when Matt would never come home again? It was not fair. Park carried on conversations in her head now. 'Buck up you selfish slob! When has anything in this life ever been fair?'

"Tome on Tonya, wet's doe pack so we tan doe." Hand in hand, the two skipped off to parts unknown.

"She'll be all right." Bruce smiled faintly.

"I don't see how you can say that. Nothing will ever be all right again."

Bruce put his arm around her shoulder. "I know how you feel. When Claire died, I felt as you do. I didn't think I would ever be able to raise Sonya by myself, but with God's grace and your help, we are doing fine."

"I have to get out of here." She clamored for fresh air.

A Mysterious Offer

She found her way back to the dark gloomy home she shared with Matt. Park was not one to sit idly by, especially during a stressful time. She needed to face Matt's ghost as soon as possible.

She found a note on her front door mat when she went to unlock the door. Enclosed in the fold was a single daisy, smiling carefree. Park could not make her face smile to match the flower. She did not want people being nice to her, just now, so she threw the innocent flower to the ground.

The widow unlocked her door, threw her keys on the stand by the door, and fell dejectedly into Matt's plush chair, again. She blew a stray hair out of her face with somewhat of a sigh, laid her head back and closed her eyes, forgetting about any letter in her hand. Deep in thoughts of how she could stay in this house, now that her life partner was not there to share it with her, Park started as a metal object fell to the floor.

Curiosity overtook her, when the culprit turned out to be a key. She opened the letter.

Dear Friend,

I have a place in Montana that sits on a private lake. It is a place of healing for me, and I thought you might find use of it now.

The cabin comes fully furnished, except food, and it is yours for the duration. There are no strings attached. I would much appreciate your visiting it. It has been deprived of a loving touch far too long. The lake is stocked, and there is great fishing this time of year. I know how you love to fish, and there is a small boat for your pleasure, if you are able.

Don't worry about a thing; no one need ever know what one friend is doing for another. I have enclosed a key and address. When you return home, keep the key. You may want to revisit it again sometime.

Hoping you find peace,

Your Friend

Park played absentmindedly with the key between

her fingers. How odd. She had not the first clue as to the writer of this letter. Of course, she couldn't go. It might be some psycho or something. Assuming her decision was final, she tossed the letter and key on the stand.

It would be easiest, if she were to go ahead and get Matt's affairs in order. She needed to stay busy, and this would eventually need to be finished. She began by packing Matt's clothes up, which she placed in the attic. Yes, someday she would probably have to get rid of them, but for now, she couldn't. This was almost harder than telling her child that he was not coming home again. She could still smell his presence and hear his laughter. "Oh Matt!" she would occasionally cry out.

All of his uniforms could go back to the base, save his dress uniform with his medals pinned in a neat row. This she put carefully in a box and placed in Sarah's hope chest in the attic. Someday Sarah and her brother or sister would appreciate having something belonging to their father.

Next, she worked her way to the study downstairs. She went through his desk leaving anything she thought she might still need in tact and disposing of the others in the proper places. This reminded her that she had to arrange for some kind of funeral or memorial.

Finally, she went through private photos and divided them between the two children for future use. These she placed in the hope chest up stairs also. The sky began darkening as Park put the last paper in order.

She heard the commotion of young children laughing and playing.

"Wait a minute girls, wipe your feet. Come back. Use the rug." Bruce was protesting. He held each one's shoulder until they had finished their duty. Unintentionally, he spotted the key and note, when he knocked into the table. "Where did this come from?" he voiced to his friend, as she came back into the living room.

Convincing Argument

"I found it on my front door when I came home earlier. It is probably some nut. Of course, I wouldn't go."

"I think you should," proposed Bruce.

"What? Do you know something about this Bruce Clayton?" she demanded.

"No. I just think that the only people that know that you need healing are your friends or Matt's co-workers. They thought a lot of him. I don't think the nut jobs would know about it yet."

"Well, if you put it that way… no, I really shouldn't contemplate this notion. What if I get out there with Sarah and go in labor. She wouldn't know what to do."

"True. It wouldn't be the best thing in the world for you to go off all alone and have a baby."

"Hold on a minute. Women have babies all the time by themselves. It is quite a common practice. Have you never heard of midwives? If you are saying I can't handle childbirth all alone you are mistaken." The challenge in her tone eased Bruce's mind. There was an inkling of her old self.

"Now Park, I didn't mean anything like that. I was simply saying that I would worry about you. As for Sarah, she is more than welcome to stay at my house, indefinitely. How many times have you and Matt took care of Sonya for me and bailed me out of a jam?"

"I don't know. I do not want to be a burden," she argued.

Bruce walked to the phone, picked it up, and dialed, "Yes, do you have a flight to Lakeside, Montana? What time? Yes, for one…non…first class. How long? Thank you. My card number is…"

Park stood bewildered for a moment. She really shouldn't even contemplate this. She rubbed her temples as she felt another migraine coming on. A house by a private lake… hmm… she would not think of getting a headache there. This sounded wonderful, but she really should not. Was this really a wise decision? She would only go for a couple of days and be home before her due date. Oh, if only Matt were here to go with her. He loved to fish. They could row out on a moonlit lake. "Stop it! Stop it! Stop it! There is no more Matt," her brain screamed at her, as her head began to pound.

"Did you hear a word I said? Yoo-hoo!" Bruce snapped his fingers to bring her back into focus. "You didn't hear a word, did you?"

"I am sorry, what were you saying?"

"Your plane leaves at one thirty tomorrow afternoon. Go pack and get ready."

"You know I do have my own means of flying?"

"I thought about that," laughed Bruce, "but then, the thought of you landing while screaming in labor made me have second thoughts."

"I am glad you are having a good time at my pregnant expense. Are you sure I should be doing this?"

"Positive. Before you leave, I'll have a number for you to call when you need a midwife. We'll leave no stone unturned."

"But, I am not sure I should put Sarah off on you that way."

"The wife and I will love it," he grinned in mischief.

Thinking aloud, Park began mumbling, "I need to call... the *wife*! Did you say wife?"

Bruce nodded his head with the grin still spread wide. "Christy and I got married today. It was a simple affair. I love her. Matt made me realize that life is too short and I should waste no time." His grin faded into a commanding officer, strong jaw expression. Using his professional tone, he ordered, "Now, hop to it! Who do you need to call?"

"Absolutely no one. I am on leave from work, so they wouldn't care. I suppose I should call, just to let them know."

"Good! Now get upstairs and pack. I am not going to let you talk yourself out of this trip."

Park left briefly to throw a few things together. She returned thoughtfully, "Bruce, you and Christy are newlyweds. You have had no honeymoon, and I am throwing an extra ragamuffin on you. I had a brilliant idea. You and Christy go to the cabin by the lake for a honeymoon, and I will watch the girls."

"You think you are so smart, don't you? Stop trying to find ways of getting out of this. You are going and that is final. Tonight you'll stay at my house, and tomorrow, you are flying to the great state of Montana."

"I can't leave tomorrow, what about Matt's memorial service?"

"Have you made any arrangements yet?" he queried.

"Tomorrow morning, 10:00, at the base."

"You'll still have plenty of time to catch your plane at one thirty."

"Bruce…"

He interrupted her protests, "You will have a two hour layover in Kentucky. You can handle that can't you?" Without waiting for her reply, he pushed her slowly to the door, yelling. "Come on girls, time to go!"

"Bruce, I need to close up the house. You know we are in the middle of hurricane season."

The old friend put his arm around the two girls, as they ran to him, "There are no storms brewing for the moment. I can come by tomorrow and do it, if you will tell me what to do."

"All the deck furnishings need to go under, and the shudders need to be locked tight."

"I think I can manage that. You are still not getting out of it. Now move!"

Death and Life

Bruce and Park arrived at the Air Force base infirmary, after depositing two sleepy little girls with Christy. "You need to talk to Simmons and Barrett, before you'll be able to find any peace of mind."

Walking down the long hall, Park's legs became heavy, as if they were made of solid iron. This must be what a person walking to the death chamber felt like. Her head had steadily increased its pounding, until she thought it would explode. She desired to run, as her breath failed to fill her lungs.

When they entered the infirmary room, Frank Simmons and Rick Barrett were in deep converse. They wore sad expressions on their faces, because they had just been talking about the colonel's heroic death. Now, it was their duty to inform their beloved Colonel's widow of his last dying breath.

Before she was completely in the room, Frank and Rick rose from their bunks, gently assisting her to the only chair in the small room. Her enlarged abdomen reminded them of her delicacy.

"Mrs. Stevens!" Rick spurt out kneeling beside her. "How are you? I mean, considering and all."

She cupped Rick's purple and black face in her hands and smiled pitifully at their bravery. Tears threatened, but she controlled them, somewhat. He could not have been more pleased, if a king had knighted him. "Tell me about it, please. Did he suffer long or hard?"

"We were in the territory for eight days before they caught wind of us. We were only three, and they were many. We all knew the chance we were taking. We honestly did not think we would get caught." Frank began the story.

"Yeah, but my bungling the job caused them to find us." Rick offered, hanging his head low.

"Listen, Brother, you need not go blaming yourself for the rest of your life. It wasn't your fault."

"You can say that," continued Rick, "I got us

caught. Colonel, he played it cool. Rank and serial number all the way. He kept us alive and encouraged us by telling us of his love for you. That would get him through most of the pain. He even prayed with us."

It was Frank's turn to tell. "They tortured him more because he was a colonel and our leader. They wanted to scare us into talking, but he never broke. Not one syllable did he utter."

Rick picked it up from there. "They thought with our leader dead, they could make us break. Thanks to Bruce and his men, we never had to find out."

"They told me he was killed two days before we got there." Bruce returned the conversation to Matt.

"But did you actually see them kill him?" she pleaded for the slight hope of mistake.

Frank slowly answered, "God help us. We saw the whole of it. You don't want the details of it, please."

Again, Rick hung his head, "Park, he knew he was going to die that day. He asked us the night before to give you a message." He went to his bed and pulled a tattered shirt from beneath the pillow. "I wouldn't let them have my shirt, because it was my last mission for Colonel, and I couldn't let him down." He pulled a dirty torn piece of cloth from his shirt pocket. There stained in blood were the words, 'I luv u 3'.

Bruce fought hard to keep back the tears showing. Park felt as if her heart would break. Even in death, he took care of her. Silence filled the room in a true memorial for Matt, with his two best friends and comrade soldiers who were with him to the end. No one loved him more than the ones in that room.

Park composed first, "Now, Rick, there is to be no more blaming yourself for anything. This is the way God planned it. You didn't make any mistakes. God used you to complete His will."

"I guess I just don't see it that way. If I was not such a bumbling idiot..."

"God is in control of all. You do not do anything without His foreknowledge. You didn't make a mistake, because God does not make mistakes," she comforted gently.

Rick continued to doubt, "How can be so calm about it? If it were me, I would want revenge on the one who caused my husband's death."

"But you did not cause his death. God says in His Word, ...*it is appointed unto men once to die, but after this the judgment:* Hebrews 9:27." Park felt like crumbling, but her smile radiated joy, "It had nothing at all to do with you. It was between him and God."

"What do you mean, after death, judgment?"

Frank answered Rick's query, "We will all stand before the Perfect God who created us and answer for the choices and actions we made here on earth. We will stand in judgment by the only Righteous One. He will read of the names in the Book of Life. If your name is not in the Book, you will be cast into an eternal bottomless lake of fire and brimstone."

"How do you go about getting your name in this Book?" he earnestly inquired.

This time Bruce answered, "You can't do a thing.

Christ did it all for you. He paid for your sins at Calvary. He shed His life's blood on a wretched cross for us. *For God so loved the world, that He gave His only begotten Son, that whosoever believeth in Him should not perish, but have everlasting life.* John 3:16. He paid the price. Romans 10 says, *"That if thou shalt confess with thy mouth the Lord Jesus, and shalt believe in thine heart that God hath raised him from the dead, thou shalt be saved. For with the heart man believeth unto righteousness; and with the mouth confession is made unto salvation.* All you have to do is believe and accept Him as your personal Savior."

"A Savior; I like the sound of that. A Savior that can save me from all the scrapes I manage to get into. What do I have to do to accept?"

"Just pray," Bruce began to pray and the rest of the room followed. When it came time for Rick to pray, he prayed in humility the sinner's prayer. Jesus Christ came into his heart, and Peace came over his face and smiled.

On the way home, Park was reveling in the newfound soul, and for the moment, had forgotten her sorrow.

The Witness

Park's headache put her in a dark slumber that
night. It was the first real sleep she had since the
news. The morning brought an alarm clock in the
form of a beautiful blue and yellow bird outside her
window, singing, without a care in the world. The
sun shown brightly, making the flowers dance around
merrily. How could everything be so carefree and
confounded happy when her world was falling apart?
It should be raining and gloomy to fit her misery.

Today was the last public obstacle she had to
accomplish. After his memorial service, she could
have her mourning in private. "Oh God, help me
through this day, I pray."

According to the code, she dressed in her Air
Force uniform for the service, borrowing Bruce's
shirt in order for it to fit over her stomach. She felt
anything but comfortable at this moment. She
brushed her waist length hair until it shown, before

neatly pinning it up in the usual style. She walked passed the full-length mirror without looking at it. Park did not like looking in mirrors, because she despised her reflection.

The small base chapel seemed overstuffed with people, to the pregnant woman. Her heart pounded to the point of restricting her breath. She graciously accepted her escort to a seat in the front with Sarah tucked neatly in her arms. She could see a large picture of Matt on a flag covered table in front of the podium. A short row of chairs lined the back of the platform. The General, Frank, and Rick occupied three of the seats. A young soldier by the name of Fox sat in another. The two others were empty. After releasing Park's arm, Bruce ascended the platform and joined the others in a vacant chair. Lastly, a uniformed man came out and filled the remaining chair. Quiet chatter commenced for a few minutes longer.

The uniformed man, who proved to be the chaplain, stood up and walked to the podium. "We are here today to commemorate Colonel Matthew John Stevens, who gave his life for his country. He was, indeed, a hero. I didn't know Col. Stevens personally, but I have here a few men that did and would like to say a few things about him."

The General stood up first with kind words about the deceased. He knew Matt and Park quite well and had been their commanding officer for years. He held the highest regard for Matt Stevens.

Then it was Frank's turn to speak. "I asked to speak today at the Colonel's memorial. I know there were probably hundreds of other men more deserving and willing than I. I thank you for the opportunity to stand before you today to reverence one of the greatest men I know. Colonel Stevens was my friend, as well as my C.O. There was the Light that shown in all that he did. He lived a testimony before all his men. We did not have to wonder where he stood. He lived well before the Lord. He served well our country." He looked straight into Park's teary eyes unable to restrain his own. "Park, he would tell us about you and him and Sarah, and we would all envy him. You shared a rare love that all men desire and only few men achieve. He didn't want to leave you. He was so excited about the new baby. He was convinced that it was a girl. Anna; that is what he called her." The soldier's voice faltered. "He went to Glory, with his family as his last thought."

Park clutched her pocket that was holding the last love letter from Matt. She had never doubted Matt's love for them. He showed his love every day.

Rick humbly stood and walked forward, next. "I am here for the same reasons as Frank, only, I am less worthy. Matthew Stevens was many things to many people. I could never repay the debt I owe him. I was lost in my sin and going to hell, and I didn't even know it. Matt witnessed to me through his actions. Glory shone all over his face. It was in his talk, in his walk, even in his posture. I didn't respond to his witness until after he died. In talking with his wife and best friend, I finally understood what it was that Colonel had. Oh boy, I got it too.

Last night, thanks to Col.'s witness, I found Redemption and Salvation for all my sins; well, more like God found me. He reached down into this big ole world, found an old slob like me, and set me free. That is what I will always remember Colonel Matthew Stevens for." Having said that, he saluted to the picture in front of him and returned to his seat.

It was a full minute before Bruce was able to stand up and another before he was able to speak. Finally, in broken voice, he began, "Matt Stevens was one of the two best friends I have ever known. Webster would have to invent new words to describe my friend. He and I met through his wife and lo and behold, a week later, I found him backing me up when a couple of roughnecks were hassling me. From that day forward, he has always been an incredible friend and brother in Christ, Matt." Bruce smiled inside, "He confided a lot in me. Park, I hope he doesn't mind me telling you this now... well, I better not, I was sworn to secrecy. If I told, I'd have to cut my tongue out." This brought a much-needed smile on Park's face. "Matt was there for me, not just in words, but in deed as well. Once he was your friend, he was your friend for life. I remember when Matt accepted Christ as his Savior. He was tired of Park and me preaching at him, and he was going to refuse it all. Then, God got a hold of his heart, and he was never the same again. Anything Matt did, he did wholeheartedly, one hundred percent, and being saved was no different. He was on fire for God. Matt Stevens loved his country, he loved his job, he loved his comrades, he loved his family, and he loved God." Turning to the picture, he lifted his hat with his final words, "Matt, old buddy, I remember my promise. See you on the other side."

The chaplain ended the service by asking Rick to lead in prayer. For such a new convert, his prayer was pitifully sweet and appropriate.

To the completion of the service, Fox now stepped to the podium singing in rich baritone, *The Star-Spangled Banner*. This was the time for two soldiers to step forward, fold the American flag, and present it to the hero's widow. Outside the bells began to toll. Seven soldiers fired off three simultaneous shots, causing several unsuspecting mourners to jump in alarm.

Park was suffocating in this crowd. Crowds made her anxious. She made haste to the door, with Sarah hardly able to keep up. Park felt almost faint.

A Quiet Getaway

Fred came out of nowhere, pushed the door open, and ushered Park from the chapel into the open air. "Are you okay, Precious? You look a little peaked."

"Oh Fred! I am so glad you came. It means so much to me."

"I couldn't help but liking the guy. I mean, he can't be all that bad, look who he picked for a wife."

"You are incorrigible, Fred." The fresh air was bringing the color back to her cheeks.

"I can attest to that." Park turned around to meet her partner's smile. Sarah began tugging at her mother's arm.

"Tum on Mommy. You gonna mits your pwane."

"I think I'll have plenty of time, if you are in charge," she stooped to kiss the little girl. "You are right, though. It is time to go. Do you see Uncle Bruce?"

"Plane? You going somewhere, Precious?"

"Yes, I am taking a little time off. By the time I get back, I should have this baby in my arms. I think this is the longest pregnancy in the world, ever," laughed Park nervously.

"May I ask where it is you are going?" inquired Nicholas politely.

"Montana," was the reply.

"Do you have folks in Montana?" He seemed unaware of the look he was receiving from Fred.

"Well, Precious, get back to work soon, I'll sure miss you. Get plenty of rest and come back healthy. Come on O'Ryan, speaking of work, let's get back to it." He lingered until he received his hug and kiss from Precious. He whispered in her ear, "Take care, and if you need anything…" he let his eyes finish his sentence.

Bruce, Christy, and Park rode in silence, listening to the two playing children, in the back. Park pondered for a last resort excuse to escape this trip. She felt it would be disrespectful to Matt. The letter had said something about a place of healing. She really needed healing right now.

These next few weeks were going to be the hardest in her life. The thought of bringing Matt's baby to their house alone frightened her. Could she ever manage to raise his children without him? Would Matt really want her running off to the unknown?

No one ate very much at the dinner table. Park picked at her food, before she went to change her clothes, while Sarah sat in a lull. Bruce and Christy tried hopelessly to keep a cheerful outlook going, and Sonya, who was incapable of understanding what was really happening, continued her natural happy chattering.

Sarah wanted here mommy to stay home. It was different from all the other times she left. Daddy did not come back, what if Mommy didn't? Suddenly, she did not feel well. Christy alleviated the girl's worries, for the time being, by explaining that when mom came back, she would bring her little brother or sister with her. It was not much, but it was enough to pacify the little girl for a while.

Much of the anxiety was relieved, when the two girls saw the airplanes coming and going. It was an awesome sight for the little ones to behold. Park still searched for a last minute escape, but the eagle-eyed Bruce gave her no option to bring it up.

"I sure hope I was right in sending her off by herself this way," said Bruce to Christy as the two watched the silver bird disappear in the sky.

The widow was on her way to the unknown, all alone. It seemed to her that she had been here before, this lonely place. Before the woman had a chance to work up a frenzy, the pilot announced they were landing in Kentucky, for the layover.

"I believe this is my seat." A young man remarked, after Park re-boarded the plane. She flashed him a polite smile and continued with her reading. "Is this your first time flying?"

The young man obviously would not be discouraged and leave her to her own thoughts. "No," she replied in annoyance.

Without hearing her reply the man continued, "Me, I've flown thousands of times. Matter-of-fact, the pilot has let me in the cockpit to help him out a couple of times," he bragged. When Park's expression showed no impression, he continued without waiting for a response, "You'd get a kick out of all those gadgets and panels. I could get the Pilot to let you up there. You're kinda pretty, I think he'd like you. I could get him to show you how this big boy runs. Would you be interested?"

"No, thank you."

"Are you sure? I think you would get a big kick out of it."

There was no getting rid of this nuisance. She curtly responded, "I have been a pilot in the United States Air Force for five years. I already know about all the panels and gadgets. Now if you'll excuse me." Stepping over him, she left before he could accumulate any more lies and found another private seat to continue in her thoughts.

Park stepped off the plane in Grandier, deeply

breathing in the clean Montana air. This is what she needed. Outside, the airport was a town lit up in grandeur.

The bus ride to Lakeside dampened her spirits, some. It was stuffy and hot, and everyone stared curiously at the pregnant woman. It was very late when she dismounted the bus in Lakeside. The only building in sight was a small general store, which had a faint light burning upstairs. She hesitated about knocking, but she knew not where she was going.

Heavy steps followed her knock on the old wooden door. A boy, about nineteen, opened up. Upon seeing Park, he grinned widely, "Yes ma'am, what can I do for ya?"

"I am on my way to this address," she presented the paper, which contained the information. "I need some groceries and directions."

"No problem, I can get you some stuff together in a hurry t'night. In the morning, I'll fix up a lot more and deliver it up to ya."

"That would be wonderful! Now, if you will point

me in the right direction, I will get started after you procure those items for me."

"It's a five mile trip. You ain't planning on walking are ya?"

"Five miles is not that much. I do not mind the walk."

He eyed her pregnant condition, "I got an ole pick-up out back. I suppose I could run ya up, no problem at all."

"That would be generous, thank you. Are you sure it is no bother."

"Jus let me git my shoes on my feet. By the way, Kevin's the name."

"Park, Park Stevens," reaching her hand out.

"Park, what kind of name's that? Kind of quirky don't ya think?"

She could not help but to laugh, "I suppose it is quirky at that."

Kevin proved to be very sweet. He talked nonstop about weather, scenery, people, anything he could think of mentioning. Park thanked him kindly, and paid him for his service. She stood before her haven, at last. It looked cozy, even in the dark. A beautiful log cabin nestled in the woods beside this even more beautiful lake.

The key slipped into the hole and quietly clicked in the latch. Opening the door displayed dozens of daisies in different colors, all leaning to greet her.

The Cabin

The fragrance filled room offered a sweet
welcome. She went from flower to flower feeling the
petals against her cheeks. Suddenly, a terrifying
thought came to her. Maybe this was a mistake, after
all. How did these flowers get here? Could it really
be some nut trying to get her off by herself? She
would ride back to the store with Kevin tomorrow
and call Bruce. Her nerves began to strain, while
wary thoughts plagued her mind.

The Montana night air was cold. Park went to the
woodpile, out by the old tractor shed, to get some
wood for the fireplace, since the cabin's only source
of heat was the fireplace. This may have been
primitive, but Park liked not being hampered with
modern conveniences.

Once the fire was going, she took a long hot bath
and climbed her weary body into the luxurious bed.
As tired as she was, a bed of nails would probably

seem luxurious. Sleep came easily for her that night.

She saw visions in her sleep of Matt running on a huge treadmill calling repeatedly, "I am coming Park, don't have her till I get there." Her eyes opened wide and her brow broke into a sweat, when he called and no sound came out. He was running vainly, reaching for her, calling for her. Oh Matt, why couldn't it have been her to die, instead? She would rather die a thousand deaths than to try to live without him.

The morning brought a happier look on things. True to his word, Kevin brought a month's supply of food and necessities up from the store. Park questioned him about to whom this place belonged, but he only shook his head and said, "Not suppose ta tell." She also questioned him about the flowers in the house. "My mom brought um up here. She gotta phone call from the one who owns this place. She followed the instructions to the letter. Why, was something wrong with 'em?"

"They were perfectly lovely. I can't help being curious, though. Who could be doing all this for me?

73

How do I know the owner is to be trusted?"

"Upon my word, ma'am, they's as honorable as they come. Would I lie ya?"

"Well, I would hope not. Here is the money for the groceries. There is a little extra for you delivering them for me."

"No need for that, it was my pleasure. There's not a lot of pretty women folk come around these parts. I like to keep my eye on 'em when they do." With a lift of his hat, he was gone.

Kevin's code of conduct was that, because of his great respect for the owner of this place, he would keep his mouth shut and blindly see to the requests of the owner. Revealing information that was supposed to be top secret would make him a yutz and Kevin Carter was no yutz.

After a successful day of fishing, Park began to prepare for the evening by gathering enough firewood to last until morning. Outside, she could smell a campfire filtering through the great woods. There was nothing like the great outdoors, sitting in front of a campfire, looking at the vast western dome filled with bright clear stars, and at sunset, some of the most beautiful colors imaginable.

Suddenly, she realized that she should get enough firewood for a couple of days. She had felt the first early twinges of that expected moment. It took three trips to make sure she had enough. The little tyke was not due for another week. Why were the contractions so severe? She doubled over in pain.

A Legacy is Born

She must prepare for what was to come next. Bruce had remembered to get the number from his friend, for a midwife, but being as she had no phone, how would that help? "O.k. God, I guess it is just You and me. I know this is not Your first time, or mine. Please, help me, I pray. Give me wisdom and strength. Matt is not here, but I sure am glad You will never leave me or forsake me."

She made a bed in front of the fire. All the cushions from the couch lay cozily on the floor, along with the pillows from the bed. She brought clean towels beside the makeshift bed. Now, for clean linens and clothes… the twinges were coming closer together and stronger now. She was ready for the drama.

Once more, she went to the bathroom to take a hot bath and lay in there until she heard a knock on the door. The pains came more frequent, and the hot water helped ease it. She dressed in a loose cotton gown as quickly as her rebelling body would allow. It took a few minutes, but she managed to get to the door.

"Hi, I am Elizabeth. You are in need of a midwife?" came a sweet as honey voice belonging to a small middle-age woman. She watched Park wrinkle her nose during another pain. "Looks like I'm just in time," she noticed.

Park's only thought was that, once again, God had answered her prayers. "Come in..." taking short breaths, "please." The woman followed her to her bed by the fire. "I don't know what else you might need."

"Looks like you were prepared to do this all on your own. I am glad you called though. Bringing new life into the world is such a wonderful miracle. I'll just go get some water. You lay down here and get as comfortable as you can."

Hours later, Anna Grace Stevens was born. She announced her own arrival with a healthy squall.

Elizabeth handed her to Park, after bathing her off. Park forgot all about her exhaustion, while she scrutinized every detail of her little girl.

She had the same shaped mouth and the same color of eyes hair as Matt. Tears rolled down her cheek. As long as she had Anna, she could never forget Matt.

Mother and daughter fell asleep around 4:30 in the morning. Elizabeth, content with the results, cleaned up. Collapsing onto the couch, she fell asleep, also.

Anna awoke Park with a gentle nudge, or it may have been a kick, to let her know she was hungry. At the next feeding time, a baby wail woke both women out of their sleep. Diaper change had come, and she wanted it now!

Elizabeth prepared a bountiful breakfast. "You have to keep up your strength."

The midwife spoke with a soft, pleasant voice that soothed the senses. Park was impressed with this woman's professionalism. Everything was orderly. While she washed the dishes, Park slipped some money in her bag. Elizabeth informed Park that she no longer needed her, and she must go home. Park thanked her and watched as she disappeared into the woods.

Once alone, Park had plenty of time to think about the mysterious midwife. How did she know the exact moment to come? How did she even know about Park being alone in the middle of nowhere? This woman appeared in the midst of her deepest need. It had to be that God sent her. Elizabeth had said that someone had called her, but Park had no means of phoning anyone. Maybe Bruce called. Being that she had no answers for these questions, she simply gave glory to the One who controlled it all.

The next two weeks proved to be a time of healing for the widow and new mother. Staying busy had always agreed with her through hard times. She bundled Anna up and took her on boat rides in the little rowboat. Hiking was a favorite, Park thrilled in showing Anna all that God had created. The good exercise was helping Park's natural shape show its former self, and the color was returning splendidly in her cheeks. Of course, Anna slept most of the time, but it did not stop her mother from talking to her.

Another batch of daisies came the day after Anna was born. This time, she found them on her doorstep. Someone had soundlessly left them there. Once again, she wondered who this flower bearer could be.

Some flowers were yellow, some pink, yet all were beautiful. Park took some, tying their ends together, made a little halo for Anna. Baby Anna did not know how pretty she looked sleeping with her crown. This would not last after she woke up, so Park had to enjoy it now.

The little cabin in Montana was very secluded. No one was about anywhere. It must be true what Kevin said about the nearest neighbor being miles away. For the first week or so, Park smelled a campfire. Maybe someone was on a hunting expedition.

She sent an informative letter home to Bruce and the gang, by way of Kevin, as he came by at the end of the first week to check on her. It was a surprise to find the baby born and that both were in good shape. Afraid lest he should damage this precious one, he politely refused the mother's plea to hold the baby.

He was amazed at how the events leading to Anna's birth had come about. He knew nothing of a phone call, nor did he know of the midwife.

Elizabeth came to see Park at the end of the first week, but Park didn't see her, because she and Anna were in the little rowboat in the middle of the lake. It took Elizabeth a few minutes to focus her eyes in order to see the baby. She saw they were both doing well and returned from whence she came, unnoticed. She felt there was no need for her to return, leaving Park to wonder if she had been but an apparition or a mirage in the desert of her loneliness.

Angels of Mercy

Park was having an enjoyable time in this magical place. Two more weeks passed in a blink of an eye, and the time to leave was nigh at hand, all too soon. So content was she at this little hideaway that she was ready to bring Sarah here so they could live the rest of their lives in unbridled bliss. Over the last weeks, she gave little thought as to who the donor of the cabin might be. Occasionally, curiosity would cross her mind, and then Anna would call for her attention causing that thought to be incomplete.

It was time to go home, so the new mom made the trip to the store in order to make the arrangements with the newborn sleeping in a crudely made papoose on her mother's bosom. The walk had exhilarated Park. Kevin's mother was alone in the store when she arrived, and her expression betrayed her surprise that a mother had walked five miles so soon after giving birth. Nevertheless, she smiled her greeting.

"Good morning," Park smiled in return.

"Morning. I see ya brought the little one."

"She is such a delight. Would you like to hold her?" Park unloaded the tiny bundle.

"Mercy me. I haven't held a baby in years. She's so little. Kevin told me aboutcha' having her up in that cabin all by yourself. I don't reckon I could do that if I had to." The older woman cherished the baby in her arms.

Park asked, "May I use your phone? I would like to call home. I am afraid I must leave this little bit of heaven and return to the real world."

"Right over beside the soda machine. You want 'er back? I'd be right pleased to hold'er till ya got done."

"Thank you, if you would. I will just be a few minutes, I hope." She left Mrs. Carter smiling down at the baby face and cooing. Park called Bruce's house first, "Hello, Christy?"

"Yes? Park!" recognizing her voice, Christy continued, "Hey how is your trip?"

"Oh it is so beautiful here. I could stay forever."

"Forever? We would miss you. You have to come back. Bruce would worry sick over you."

"I would miss you, too. Unfortunately, I am coming home. I'm getting ready to call the airlines to book a flight."

"When, exactly, should we expect you home?"

"I am not sure specifically, but it will be in the next few days. How is Sarah?"

"She's fine. She and Sonya are having a blast. You know, she misses her mommy and daddy a lot."

"I miss her, too." There was sadness that entered her tone at the mention of Matt that cut to the kind heart on the other end of the receiver. "Is she excited about meeting her baby sister?"

"Oh yes! She and Sonya are already planning to baby-sit, while you take a hot bath or read a book or something. It is so adorable," laughed Christy on the other end of the line.

"That sounds wonderful to me. I couldn't find two better people to love and watch her than our two girls. Well, give them my love, hugs, and kisses. I will be home very soon."

"Call back with the airline information, so Bruce will know when to pick you up at the airport."

"Don't bother Bruce about that. I will come over, as soon as I get back, to get Sarah and Sonya."

"Now Park, you know he'll be mad at us both if you do not..."

"I mentioned to Bruce about the two of you taking a honeymoon when I get back," interrupted Park covertly, "so pack Sonya's necessities. We have her toothbrush, pajamas, and a few clothes at our house. Just use your judgment on what she needs."

"Park, don't do this to me. I don't want to argue."

"There is no argument, Dear. Make sure Bruce is taking next week off."

Christy knew she could tell her new husband all she wanted, but he would do what he would do. If he didn't want to take off from work, all the asking in the world wouldn't change his mind. "I do not know if that is possible, with everything that has been going on. Bruce wouldn't want to impose on you."

"My foot, like it would be an imposition. I will call the base myself and see that he does. All right, I'll see you soon. Love to all. Bye."

"Park, don't do anyth..." the dial tone screamed in her ear.

Park phoned General Kincaid at the base. After explaining her intent, he was all too happy to accommodate her.

The Request

Finally, she called her partner. "Partner! It has been a long time, since I called you that. I assume I am still your partner."

"Park! I declare! Where in the world are you?" came the cheerful, confident voice of Nicholas.

"Still in Montana."

"Bruce called Fred with the news. You finally had her, huh?"

"Yes. She is absolutely beautiful." Park stated proudly.

"If she is anything like her mother, I know she is. Hey, when are you coming back?"

"That is the reason I was calling. I have a huge favor to ask; that is if you are not busy, or have an assignment."

He responded promptly, "Shoot. Any time I can be a white knight, I am there."

"This is a biggie. Are you sure you do not mind?"

"Just name it."

"We have a chopper in the hangar at the base. Matt bought it for me a while back. I would like a ride home. I was not too fond of the idea of riding a bus to the nearest airport and getting on a crowded plane."

"Say no more, your white knight will come, not riding on a horse, but flying a chopper, to your rescue." He was pleased to hear her laugh with him.

"I don't want anyone to know anything about this."

"No problem. What shall I do?"

"If you go to my house and lift up the hatch in the deck, you should find all my deck furniture. The blue chair has a hollow leg and taped inside, is a spare key to the house. In the right top drawer of my desk in the study, you should find all the things you need in an envelope marked *Dixie's Pride*. You shouldn't have any trouble with the guys at the hangar as long as you have all those papers. I don't think the owner of this wonderful place would mind you landing it beside the lake. It would help me out so much. In addition, my Jeep keys should be on top of my desk in the little holder, would you mind driving that so we have a ride home. The car seat is already in place. Am I asking too much of your generosity?"

"It is done. The only problem I find is that I am out on assignment for two days starting tomorrow. Can I come as soon as I get back or would that be too late?"

"That would be perfect. Thank you so much. Are you sure you don't mind?"

"Do not worry about a thing. You better give me the coordinates, though."

Park gave him the coordinates. After hanging up the phone, she second-guessed her decision of having asked him for this request.

Mrs. Carter was reluctant to give back the perfect baby. She lingered over her sleeping face, prolonging the visit. Over an hour since entering, Park emerged from the store, having completed all her tasks.

Nicholas was at home, when he received Park's phone call. Once he returned the receiver, he hurriedly mounted his motored steed to fulfill his promise.

At the Stevens' house, the blue chair was easy to find. The key was exactly where she said it would be. He entered her house as if it was the sacred abode of a heavenly creature. If he dared breathe, it could possibly defile this seemingly holy place. His steps were gentle through the kitchen and into the den where he could see the stairs.

He knew where the study was, because Matt had taken him in there one time. The things he needed were right there where his partner said they would be. He looked in the paper clip holder on top to find the prophesied keys.

The house smelled clean. Even down to the papers on her desk, the place appeared in immaculate order. He contemplated opening the shutters, but decided to wait until he returned from his assignment and was on his the way to serve his knightly duties. He pocketed the key for his return.

He pondered the idea he wanted some flowers or balloons or some kind of welcome when she returned home. Park covered it well in her conversation, but she was still mourning for the loss of her husband. Anything Nicholas could do to help her, he was willing to do.

His feelings for Park were of deep loyalty and friendship. Most people instantaneously fell in love with Mrs. Stevens' charm the second they met her. One can tell a lot about another in their friendships and kinships, and Park was an incredible person. She was gracious, modest, and kind to a fault.

This was to be his partner for a long time. He had better let her come to trust him as well. If she couldn't depend on him in small favors, then how could she trust him when her life was in danger? He desired to gain the respect and loyalty of his partner.

Snowbound

A successful mission rewarded Nicholas with an early reprieve. Now, he could go rescue his partner.

He made a detour to the florist on the way to Park's house, ordering flowers and two dozen balloons for immediate delivery. He proceeded to her house to open the shutters and windows to allow freshness to blow in.

In fifteen minutes, the delivery girl knocked on Park's door and handed Nicholas his order. He awkwardly arranged them in various places throughout the house. The partner wanted to take the balloons to the nursery for the baby, but afraid to venture where he should not, he left them in the den. Pleased at his accomplishment, he took one last look at the vast sea of gladiolas mixed with wildflowers before leaving for the Air Force base hangar.

At his arrival, only one man was visible. He was inside tinkering with a small plane. Nicholas asked him which of the two aircrafts belonged to Park Stevens. With a curious eye, the young man pointed to the blue and silver one.

After showing the proper paperwork to the man, Nicholas was on his gallant quest. There were refueling points on the journey, which put him in the Montana skies late that evening.

Snow had begun to blow past him a while ago, and with every kilometer, it came down thicker and stronger. The further he flew the poorer his visibility became. Maybe he should land here. Park wasn't expecting him until tomorrow, so if things got bad...if things got bad! There was no way to contact her. She was in the middle of nowhere, with a month-old baby, alone. He decided it was better to fight his way to his partner in this storm. The hour flight turned out to be a several hours. At last, he approached the exact coordinates and fought to land the magnificent beast without sitting her on a tree or the house.

Jumping from the whirring bird, he landed in at least seven-inches of snow that covered his rudders beyond sight. He drew his lightweight coat closer around his neck, trying to see which way to go.

Having heard sounds, Park had awakened, looking at the clock. It was 2:20 a.m. as the sound came nearer. Then, she recognized the sound. Rolling away from Anna, she slipped to the cold floor with her bare feet, threw on the man's bathrobe she had found in the cabin, and ran to look out the window. She could not see anything yet, so she stoked the fire and put another log on. Nicholas was not supposed to be here until tomorrow, but that surely sounded like *Dixie's Pride*.

Perhaps that was someone else; maybe the lunatic whose cabin she had been using freely had her at his vantage and had come to complete his deed. Amidst these thoughts, a blinding light penetrated the window. It was Nicholas! Park watched the bird contrarily lower to the white blanket.

White blanket! It had been snowing! When did that start? When the ignition stopped its humming, she threw herself out the door into the cold Montana snow to meet the first person from home she had seen in a long time.

"What on earth?" she heard her partner speaking loudly over the wind. "What are you doing out here with no shoes on?" Reaching her side, he tried to lift and carry her, but she had run deftly back to the house.

"Come on in to the fire," he barely caught, for the wind almost ripped the words from her lips.

He stomped the snow from his boots before entering. Park had run ahead to put on a kettle for cocoa. To the man she appeared angelic, almost dancing on her toes from the kitchen.

She returned, "I put some cocoa on for you. Here, let me take your coat. You sit here by the fire and get warm." She shook the remainder of water from his coat and hung it to dry in front of the fire.

"Someone told me it would be cold here, but I was not prepared for snow. All I brought was this flimsy thing that won't keep anything warm."

"This is the first snow of the year, too," her eyes

twinkled merrily in the firelight. She looked like a little girl on Christmas morning awaiting her presents, "there are some clothes in the bedroom that would probably fit you. Hold on," she vanished.

Nicholas could hear water running while he rubbed his hands into the fireplace to get the feeling back. Shortly Park returned, still smiling. "I ran you a hot bath and put some clean clothes in there. You better warm up and get clean, or you will catch your death. The hot cocoa should be ready by then."

"Me, what about you? You were the one out in the snow barefoot."

"I am used to it. Now, go before the water gets cold."

He obediently followed his partner's order. The hot water hit the spot, and all too soon, it had comforted his weary bones, and he emerged feeling like a new man. Park brought him a tray, laden with delectable soup, homemade cornbread, and a cup of steaming cocoa. He had forgotten, during the trial of the storm that he had not eaten since the noonday meal. Food had evaded his attention in desire to get to his destination.

Park smiled, "Those clothes are a perfect fit."

He heartily ate the food that Park laid before him in royal fashion. Park warmed his soul with her smile and tried to warm his body by wrapping blankets about him.

"How bad was the flying?" queried his hostess.

"It got worse closer in. Visibility is impossible."

"I guess that means we can't leave tomorrow," Nicholas could not quite tell if her voice sounded a little anxious or a little relieved.

"Partner, this means we will not leave for a couple of days."

Leaving Paradise

"Do you mind being holed up with your partner for a couple of days? If I had known this snow storm was going to hit today, I would have made a way to come sooner, somehow."

Park just smiled her lovely smile as usual, "We have spent more than a few days together before, and not in such a lovely abode as this. I assume that we will spend many more, on the job. The question is can you put up with us?"

"A baby is a new experience for me, but I think I can handle just about anything as opposed to that storm outside."

"Then it's settled," she left to attend to Anna who had wakened.

When she returned a while later, Nicholas had devoured every last morsel. He never knew leftovers could be so delicious. She introduced him to the small package that went by the name, Anna. He sat there staring at the delicate limbs, afraid to touch the fragile little person lying in his arms.

The natural paternal instincts kicked in for Nicholas O'Ryan. He matured in another dimension instantaneously. When he had children, he would understand the responsibility and love, because of what he went through on this day. Suddenly, he began worrying and asking all kinds of questions: "Is she too cold?", "Is she hungry?", or "She will not get sick in this weather, will she?" Park laughed her charm at his sweet innocent ignorance. She did like the way he was trying to father them both.

An exhausted Park showed the guest to the main bedroom, and the three retired for the rest of the night.

Nicholas slept late, whereas Park was up with Anna a short time later. It was the second time she awoke, since they went to bed, that she decided to stay up and prepare breakfast. Before long, the ambrosial aromas of bacon, hash browns, eggs, and toast wafted in to the sleeping guest, bringing him to his full senses. He arose to find his own clothes returned to him, cleaned, ironed, and smelling fresh.

After dressing and making the bed, the guest cautiously stepped into the kitchen. The table was set to perfection. It was an inviting vision to this man, who had never seen such a table in his home. He had seen this kind of etiquette at restaurants, but it was a treat to have this personal service at home.

He quickly made his trip to freshen up, and Park was putting juice on the table when he returned the second time. She smiled at him with grace, asking if he slept well. No eating facility could have prepared a better meal than was laid before him. He ate until his stomach could hold no more.

Nicholas pleasured in helping her with kitchen duty. The two looked as if they had been doing this all along. They took a brief walk out on the small porch to view the status of the snow. The wind had blown snow up under the brief canopy, which put it already past their knees and still coming vigorously.

They quickly hopped out to the woodpile, but

Nicholas refused to allow Park to carry in one stick. He made a second and third trip out to ensure they had enough to get them through the next couple of days.

On his last trip up, Kevin had brought enough supplies to last Park longer than her intended stay, so they were set for the storm. It was just like being on assignment, except they were in no danger or pretending to be something they were not. This was good medicine for Park. It was helping her to forget her grief and sorrow.

The only communication with the outside world was the battery operated radio which announced the storm should be over and roads passable within two days. They deduced the skies should be passable before the roads.

Nicholas had his phone with him, but the batteries were dead. Exiled, he felt no need for the outside world. He was in the presence of angelic deity with no want for disturbance. No one had ever taken care of him like this. How could a mere acquaintance make him feel more loved, appreciated, or at home, than the woman who had raised him all his life?

This woman had the power to entrance all people to succumb to her every wish. She was definitely beautiful, and not just topically. Her splendor radiated from the inner depths of her soul and mere flesh and bone could not contain it. Her voice was delicate, yet, on proper occasion, commanding. Her golden brown hair flowed clinging around her waist, while a few young curls framed her petite face. He could certainly see what Matt Stevens had seen in this exquisite specimen of womanhood. Ah, Matt… barely cold in his grave, and Nicholas was admiring his wife. He was a heel!

Two days flew by for Nicholas, and shamefully, he did not want the storm to go away. However, duty called without patience.

He dug out the rudders and tested the chopper to see if she would fly carefree. Upon finding that she did, they closed up the cabin for a long winter's sleep and headed home.

Homecoming

The sweetest fragrance permeated her humble dwelling, when Nicholas opened her door. Stepping inside, the most gorgeous and abundant wealth of gladiolas and wildflowers she had ever seen greeted her gladly. She caught her breath when her eyes fell upon the balloons floating like a merry-go-round; some drooping slightly from the length of time that had elapsed, but most were merrily clinging to the ceiling. She saw her partner's 'guilty as charged' expression and broke into a radiant smile.

"You did all of this," she turned completely around twice and added, "for us?"

He grinned timidly, "I wanted you to feel missed. I hope you do not mind the liberty I took with your key." He reminded Park of a little shy schoolboy.

"Oh, it is so...look at all the beautiful colors. Look at them proudly cascading their perfect silken cups. It is all so... Oh, Nicholas, you shouldn't have, but

103

oh! I do feel missed, and there are balloons for Anna, all pink and pretty." The light dancing in Park Steven's eyes was all the thanks her partner and friend needed. It pleased him to please her.

The escort placed her bags inside at once. Park took the sleeping Anna to her new crib. Nicholas gathered all the strings belonging to a balloon, and following the mother, gave them their freedom once more. They made sure she was safely tucked away in dreamland before both leaned over to give her one last goodnight kiss.

Nicholas insisted on distributing Park's suitcase to its proper place. He deliberately averted his eyes from seeing anything except the floor in front of him. Desecrating her sacred inner chamber would be irreparable treason, so he quickly retreated down the stairs to safety.

Shortly thereafter, they exchanged goodbyes and debts of gratitude, before Nicholas thrust himself back into his own cold, lonely world.

Corporal Nelson had directed the landing of their

helicopter at the Charleston Air Force base. He thought it not strange to say something to Clayton when passing him in the hall about seeing Park's new baby.

With the realization that his best friend had snuck in unawares, Bruce's mind set about to surprise her in return. He called Christy to fill her in on the details of his scheme.

After Christy picked Bruce up from work, the four hungry souls burst through Park's front door, showing the traveling wayfarer how much they missed her and demanded to see the new addition to the fold and to know where all the flowers and balloons came from.

Anna had to awaken and put on a show for her fans when she knew they were all watching. Sarah fell in love immediately with her sister. She and Sonya kept running gentle fingers over her soft fuzzy head.

Bruce searched to see if any sadness lingered hauntingly in Park's eyes, but only an occasional flicker crossed the otherwise twinkling eyes. No one could expect Park to forget her soul mate, but he did want his friend to suffer as little as possible for her loss. He did notice that the baby seemed to be a balm for her soul.

Christy watched Bruce watch Park with a touch of envy for the bond these two shared. This was something she would never have in common with either and sometimes felt a little on the outside. Should she tell either Bruce or Park? Both would move heaven and earth to remove her discomfort. Her husband loved her, and she would have to learn to accept that his best friend was a woman. She knew this before she married him, and promised herself never to let this bother her, but she was only human. Park had never done anything inappropriate, but Christy feared that Matt's absence might change things. Maybe part of what made her feel this way was the fact that Bruce was married and had a life before she ever came along. He even had Sonya without her. Was there anything he actually needed from her?

"Penny for your thoughts," Bruce stole up behind his fair maiden as she stood staring out over the ocean from the deck.

"Oh, just a little jealous, I suppose," she sighed, resting in his strong arms,

"My fair lady, what in the world could you possibly have to be jealous about? You are the most gorgeous lady and are married to the most handsome man in the world, might I say." He was motioning to himself with his hands.

A rare smile covered her sweet lips, "What have I to offer you? You have all this without me. I would like to contribute something to this marriage."

"Oh, is that all? Okie dokie, bear me more children woman," he scowled a savage he-man roar. "Fifteen or sixteen more'll do. Rooooar!"

"I don't think so. You might need a whole slew of wives for that job."

"Then how about giving me two more?"

"Do you really want more, or are you simply

trying to appease me?"

"Woman, do you not know a man's pride is his children. I want me a boy to carry on the Clayton name. All I have is Sonya, and she will get married and change her name to something like Butkis, or Mrs. Seymour Butts. Just think, my daughter, Mrs. Offleburger! The shame of it all! Give me children woman, boy children!" He pulled her within his embrace.

"This view is so incredible, isn't it?" Christy broke the silence.

"The view sure is incredible," Bruce murmured in her ear, but his eyes were on his bride, not the ocean.

Sonya came up behind pulling on her dad's shirt. "Daddy, Pawuk wonts me to spend duh week wif hurwa. Tan I doe?"

"We'll see," he answered as he turned to reenter the house to confront his best friend. "Park, Kincaid informed me that as of Friday evening, I am on a forced leave. It seems that he found out I got married, somehow. Do you know anything about that?"

"Now, why in the world would you think I would know something about that? I arrived home not just three hours ago, and trust me; you were not the first thing on my mind."

"Don't try to pull the wool over my eyes, Friend. I talk to my wife, who tells me everything, and she told me a funny little story about a phone call she received by a one Park Stevens. Do you still disclaim any information?"

"I do."

"I don't believe you for a second. I don't know what to think about you and Kincaid ganging up on me this way. I will not forget this, Missy."

"Friday, huh?" she smiled mischievously, with the plan already set, "It is wonderful that Kincaid is letting you off so soon after your wedding. I planned on going to the mountains for the weekend, and Sonya will spend the night tonight and go with us."

"You think you are clever. You are a sly dog, that is what you are, a sly dog. Have you also picked out where you intend us to go?"

Park gave Christy a crafty smile, "That ball is in your court, Sister."

"I have always wanted to go to Niagara Falls, could we manage that?" she began to get excited.

"Then to Niagara it is." Bruce threw a, 'charge to war', fist in the air. "We bid you adieu Miss Park, we will be taking our leave now, but don't think I have forgotten your dirty little tricks, Missy." She received a hug and kiss on the cheek from each one of her guests.

"I'll see you tomorrow, and bring Sonya's things to stay the week."

Once the children were asleep and Park found a few minutes of solitude while feeding Anna, Matt's memory fell hard on her mind. She sat in the dark silence facing a lonely house without him.

Forgetting Paradise

The morrow bore a glorious crown of sunshine, along with an unusual heat wave for late October.

The weather in Charleston was almost as pleasant as the aura. The great city held a charm that one could only describe as a magnolia blossom pressed in the pages of time from years gone by, when wealthy young beaus courted the beautiful southern belles, and the ravages of the Civil War had not placed their cold bitter hands upon her delicacy. The magnetic beauty of the old weathered mansions, that over the years kept royalty, like Prince Charles from England, would unfold their bounty for whoever might appreciate what they had to offer.

Nevertheless, the drastic change in temperature was already working its ugly effect on the two wanderers from afar. Park was the first to show signs of a cold, but she did not let that hinder their trip to the North Carolina mountains.

111

There was a need to return to the little church up there that few really understood. It was a haven of rest for the weary. It was the one place in the whole world where Park could have a mending fellowship with her Lord and Master. She had a regular church in Charleston, but none could compare to this one. Now, she needed God's touch and comfort, and she felt this was the only place she would find it.

The old familiar sanctuary did not fail Park, either. As her feet touched the front steps, the power of God moved filled her spirit. It had been over two months since she and Matt had been to church. Her and Matt; yes, the last time she was here, he was by her side, now she was rendered a widow.

As usual, the pastor asked her if she would sing, but she declined on the excuse of her cold, but agreed to play a song on the piano. Her music was rolling from her heart, and she forgot, for an instant, that anyone was listening, and simply played for the memory of Matt, *The Old Rugged Cross*. There was no preaching. It became one of those services where most cannot sit still without popping up to give testimony for what the Lord has done for them. This was a new experience for both Sonya and Sarah. They wanted to giggle and talk about what these crazy people were doing, but with stern looks from Park, they stifled that desire.

The night service proved to be as Spirit-filled as the morning, replenishing Park with the Spiritual food in which her soul famished.

Nicholas was plagued with the sneezing and running nose to the point that they sent him home from work on Monday.

The boss gave him a brief on Park's and his assignment, which they would begin next week. He took it to her to familiarize herself with it.

He arrived early Monday morning to find no one at home, because they had stayed an extra night in the mountains. Finally, on Wednesday, he caught up with her. Park conveyed her appreciation for all his help in getting her and Anna home. She did not feel comfortable giving him a hug, so she offered her charming smile of gratitude, though her nose shone red. After he left, she was glad she had reacted so.

Nicholas held her in aloofness. It was back to business with him; almost as if it had all been a vision that only she could remember. Nicholas O'Ryan was the best at his job for one very simplistic reason. He did not allow his feelings to become a liability. Once an agent allowed that to happen, they were no longer good for service.

He had forgotten this and lost some of that while snowbound in the west, but the home ground brought him to his senses. He was generally quiet and extremely professional, but with a partner like his, one could not so easily maintain that rapport. He decided to further his distance and see less of her on the outside in case he let her kindness to him become his weakness. He had never shared with anyone a personal relationship, and he could not afford to begin now. That is how he has stayed alive this long, that and the merciful hand of God.

By the time both agents appeared for duty, only a remnant of their colds lingered. They suffered a little teasing by Fred, because the two were simultaneously sick. Nicholas proved his loyalty by keeping their exodus from the snowstorm private.

Bruce and Christy returned from their journey wearing happy smiles and adoring glances for one another, while Sonya fairly commanded she wanted a baby sister, too.

With orders to report for duty on Tuesday, Park had mixed feelings about returning to the long missions. When hard times had come in the past, she had a tendency to immerse herself in work. She could accomplish recuperation, as well as becoming a better agent through losing her identity.

However, Anna had changed everything. It would be torturous leaving a two-month-old overnight. Since Matt was gone, she had to be mom and dad, and that meant she would need to stay closer to home. With these thoughts, she requested her assignments be short for the first few months.

Pretenders

Richardson gave her a light load the first several months. He knew it would be a long time before she would be complete again, so he sympathized with her needs.

Her first long assignment came a few months later. She and Nicholas were to pose as man and wife in order to bring down a baby-selling ring that the FBI had been after for a while. The kidnappers, suspecting the FBI was onto them, moved their cartel to the Florida coast, which gave them easy access to exiting the country in flight.

As Mr. and Mrs. Wilson, the agents would go to any length to get a baby, because the wife had been in a mental institution for a while, causing the courts to refuse adoptive custody. Richardson, with Zoe's help, had fabricated the Wilsons a history that was both viable and untraceable.

They rented a house for continuity, which they

assumed would be under surveillance by the perpetrators, but everything must appear legit. If they messed up this time, they would lose their last chance to catch these horrible people.

Flight 706 carried Mr. and Mrs. Wilson to the meeting. Nicholas, in the role of Frank Wilson, had already made the initial call to get the ball rolling. The plan was to meet the person or persons for an interview, once they arrived in Florida.

Zoe informed Richardson that someone was searching the background on Mr. Wilson, Executive Vice President of a major corporation. They programmed the system so that when anyone investigated, they would come directly through headquarters. Per his orders, Zoe added a three point two million dollar bank account and the medical records on Mrs. Wilson, who had run into some health problems early in life, leaving her barren. In addition, they included other medical info, such as the mental state of Mrs. Wilson as being dangerous to herself.

The meeting was set for nine fifteen in the evening, at a questionable Palm Springs bar. They arrived as early as they dared without arousing suspicion. Hand in hand, they walked into the den of iniquity, portraying a nervous innocent couple frightened to be in a place like this. Mrs. Wilson became more edgy than normal to fulfill her insanity ploy.

A husband on her arm did not stop a couple of drunken stupid men calling vulgar things toward Park's direction. It was enough to set Mr. Wilson off without recourse, but he had to keep up appearances. She clung to him to appear dependant and weak. Her gentle manner discreetly soothed the anger beast within her mate. "It will be over soon," she whispered to him.

They knew the person they were meeting would put them to the test, before he would reveal too much about himself. They also knew that if they passed it too well, then he would get suspicious.

Unbeknownst to the two agents, the man they

were looking for was watching them from a smoky dark corner. He sent a scantily clad barmaid to them to show them the way to his table. He may have shot them right there for all the expression he revealed to them.

"Wilsons, I presume. Greer's the name," he did not offer to shake their hand.

"Yes, I am Frank, and this is my wife, Evelyn," Nicholas' voice was soft and weak. The stench of the man's cheap cologne was stinging Park's nostrils. She shuddered at the thought that this man had access to any child. His oily cowardice voice sickened her even more than the cologne to the point she felt dizzy. Nicholas had continued, using this to his advantage. "Please excuse my wife. She has not been well lately. She wants a child so bad, it unnerves her to the point she needs help sometimes. That will not hurt our chances of getting one, will it?"

"I understand. Maybe we can help you adopt one and put your mind at ease, Evelyn." He smiled at her with a wicked smile. She had seen smiles like that before on the devil's spawn. This was going to be harder than she thought. She wanted to take him out and beat the living daylights out of him, but she had to stay in her roll. "Now I know you ain't picky," he was saying, "it don't matter the color does it?"

"Oh, no!" piped up Mrs. Wilson in a whispered hush, "any little baby will do. My husband wants a little boy, but I would be just as happy with a girl."

"I think we may have one. It's a little half-breed kid, half Korean, half something else, can't really tell. She's two weeks, and we want to place her with fine folk as yourselves."

"That is wonderful, isn't it dear?" Evelyn looked eagerly at her husband. "How soon can I have my little girl, Mr. Greer? You can't imagine how long we have wanted a baby, and have been unable to get one."

"Well, now, Mrs. Wilson, Eve, it'll take a couple of weeks for the preliminaries. This isn't the easiest process to go through, you know. A deep and thorough investigation into your history has to be made, to make sure you are suitable clients for us. I'm not the only one you have to impress. I do answer to others." In reality, what he was saying was, 'I'm going to double check and then triple check your background and make sure you're not undercover cops.'

"Oh, goodness, do we have to meet anyone else? I do hate to be around a lot of people. They make me nervous," Park looked around the room as if to be paranoid.

"I'm afraid so. We don't want anyone unsuitable for our babies, so you both have to be approved by every member of our team," he actually reached his hand out to comfort her. She recoiled and tightened her hand around Mr. Wilson's arm, acting sad that she may not get the expected child if others had to approve of her.

Mr. Wilson was ready to get this lady out of this underworld of drunks and thugs. "Just name the time and place. We'll be there, and please, let's not have another meeting at this kind of place. My wife is very fragile, and this might push her over the edge."

"We'll contact you for the when and where. Meantime, don't go telling anybody that you're going to get a kid. I mean it, Evelyn, not one word. Who knows what you might slip and tell them under a little curiosity? I hesitate to work with someone so nervous and jumpy, so prove to me that you can keep your mouth shut. Frank, when you meet Harris, you do all the talking, let your wife sit back and shut up. Now, get out of here, I'll contact you soon."

The fresh air hit Park in the face, reviving her. When they got 'home', she showered twice to exorcise her body from that abominable tavern. Yet, that contaminated air was in her lungs, leaving her feeling sin stained.

They would do a sweep of the place tomorrow for hidden devices that might betray their husband and wife act. They searched nonchalantly for hidden cameras, but found none. It was doubtful these people had the sophistication or resources to manage sneaking cameras in, while they were out, but they just had to be careful.

Under the idea that the adversary was listening, Park and Nicholas put on an act of changing into their bedclothes and going to bed. Truthfully, they maintained their full apparel, and Nicholas climbed into a makeshift bed on the floor beside the bed.

What would they do if these lowlife people had the sense enough to put cameras in? They could no longer separate themselves without suspicion. Park sent up a little prayer of thanks to her Protector.

The next morning, Nicholas rose to the aroma of bacon with an extra blanket tucked fitly around him. He was not at all stiff from sleeping in the floor. He had a history of sleeping on a hard floor, even in the Marines, the cots were barely better. He made a hasty act of getting his clothes on and freshening up before hungrily going into the kitchen.

Since Nicholas had been able to 'tag' Greer the night before, Zoe and Richardson made quick progress of the short morning and afternoon.

Because of this, they were able to find his base of

operation and concluded that Greer was not the Big Guy in charge, only a hired goon that accomplished the Big Guy's requirements. It was imperative that they get the Big Guy, as well as all information stored about his whole operation, so they could return as many children as possible to their parents.

While Park was out shopping for the afternoon as Mrs. Wilson, the saleslady at the department store, which was actually an undercover agent, informed her of the progress. Park hoped that meant they would be heading home soon.

Mr. Wilson called to inform his wife that his boss, another agent, had just insisted on his and his wife's appearance for dinner that evening. They had to make it as real as possible in order to appear legit.

She showered and put on the required make-up for the farce, and tied the long tendrils in a neat pile and hid them with the wig of her disguise. Lastly, she pulled on the satin gown that clung to her ample figure uncomfortably. Tiny satin slippers and a lace shawl to cover her bare arms completed her ensemble.

When Nicholas entered his 'home' around five thirty, he could not breathe, for the sight of her took it from him for the second time. That was the moment in his life where he vowed his service to her for life. No matter what may come, he was devotedly in her league. He did not realize the truth about his feelings, because he was completely unaware that he could have such feelings.

Throughout the dinner, Mr. Wilson could not avert his eyes from Mrs. Wilson. The men, who were watching from the sidelines, fully believed this marriage was real, for Mr. Wilson had the look in his eyes as if he would move mountains for his beloved wife.

The Sting

Almost a week of sleeping on the floor passed before they heard from Greer again. During that time, they swept the house and found several listening devices planted in diverse rooms, so the charade had to continue. This assignment was beginning to look long and drawn out, and Park was ready for this operation to climax, so she could return to her children. Each day that passed grew harder for her to be away, but she never let it show outwardly.

The call from Greer came to set up a meeting with two of the partners. Whether either one would be the Big Guy, was anybody's guess.

At the meeting, Greer introduced them to a fellow named Norris and a hateful looking woman named Greta. She might have been fairly attractive to look at had she not those hard lines of years gone by on her stolid face. Neither of these were the Big Guy, but as the good Lord provides for His own, they found out who the head criminal mastermind of this whole stinking mess was. His name was Gregory Hunt.

Park entered the restroom prior to the meeting to take something to relieve her head that was pounding in rhythm with her heartbeat. A woman talking quietly on a phone, asked for Gregory Hunt. Park hastened to leave as not to eavesdrop. "How much longer, boss..." The door shut out the rest of the conversation from her earshot.

Much to Mrs. Wilson's surprise, Greer introduced her to the caller in the restroom, a few minutes later at the table. Greta grew nervous, when she found out her 'chump' had heard her phone call.

Later, she mentioned it to Greer, who seemed to think Mrs. Wilson was a simpleton and would never know the difference. However, he decided to expedite this case. He filled in the events to Hunt who agreed to move forward quickly.

Ten o'clock the next morning, Evelyn Wilson opened to a knock on her door. Greer and another man greeted her gruffly, running a detector around her body.

"We've decided to give you the kid, but we gotta make sure you're clean." Greer sneered. Turning to his companion, "She's clean."

"Only there's a condition," the other man was a handsome man, maybe in his late twenties.

She quivered her voice, "Of course, anything you say. You mean you are really going to let me have a child? What must I do?"

Greer explained the rules, "We will go now to your bank to get the money we need for expenses. When we return here, your kid'll be here with Greta."

"I will call my husband and have him meet us down there."

"No!" stormed the young man.

"What Mr. Hunt means, Evelyn, is that we're not completely comfortable with your husband being around. We want to deal with you and only you, that is, if you have access to the funds needed. This is going to be the last time you see the four of us. You may never contact any of us again."

Mr. Hunt! They had a visual. The enemy may have listening devices in this house, but so did the good guys, and upon hearing this information, the ball began to roll. Richardson deployed teams of agents to the Wilson house to apprehend Greta at the proper time, plainclothes agents infiltrated the bank, and backup followed Park. They now had proof that Norris and Greta were the ones actually stealing the babies and Hunt was the pusher. Greer, having a background in law, was the front man.

"Anything you say, he'll be so happy to find our little baby when he gets home from work. Let me get my purse." Park discreetly swept her gun into her purse in one effortless motion.

The two men sat in the front seat talking in low tones so that she could not hear the words. Occasionally, they would throw her a question or two. Park skillfully played the part of someone with a nervous condition. She bit her nails nervously and stared all around in a world of paranoia. Her captors needed no more convincing.

At the bank, she received further instruction from Greer, "You and Mr. Hunt are going in as separate customers. He will be watching you, so don't get scared and act the fool. You are to withdraw three million dollars, cash. Tell them you are investing or something. Turn around and walk out. Can you handle that, Evelyn? Because if you can't, forget ever getting a kid."

She held her head down, "I...I think I can. Three million, is it going to cost that much for expenses?"

"Do you want the stupid kid or not?" roared Greer impatiently.

She cowered fearfully, "Yes, I do."

"Good," said Hunt, "Let's go."

Park followed Greer's instructions. The undercover agents in the bank hesitated about giving up this much money, in order to appear real. No bank would readily give out three million dollars without questioning it. The 'manager' pulled her over to talk her out of it. In the end, Mrs. Wilson walked out with her cash in a briefcase.

She waited with Greer in the car until Hunt came back out. Both men sighed in relief, as did Evelyn. Acting a little excited, she confided, "That was kind of fun, I'm really starting to enjoy this a little. Are we going to my baby now?"

"No, we have a little stop to make first. I hope you don't mind." Hunt's eyes gleamed wickedly.

"We have to go pick up Norris and close up a few things. With that three million dollars in your hand, we can afford to retire permanently." Greer seemed to be loosening his tongue a bit. Park wondered if they meant to kill her, why else would they be giving her all this incriminating information?

As they pulled up to a local business office building, Hunt left Greer in the car with Park and exited. "Stay here and watch her, I'll get Norris, erase all the files, and be back in about half an hour. You'll see your baby then, Mrs. Wilson. You see, I can't afford to let you go until we are safely out of the country. I'm afraid of what you might tell people. You understand, don't you?"

"Of course," she shrunk in an act of fear.

She watched the door close to the office building, counted to twenty, and reached her trained hand forward and put the point of her gun to Greer's temple. "Take a walk with me Mr. Greer."

Nicholas, part of the backup unit, picked up the signal and was by her side in a flash. Two other agents took Greer off in handcuffs. Park pulled off her disguise, letting her golden brown hair fall freely.

Two clients walked into the office and asked for Mr. Hunt's office.

"Top floor room B," smacked a bubblegum chewing secretary.

"Thank you."

They mounted the stairs two at a time. They could hear male voices on the other side of the closed door. Without knocking, the two entered the office, receiving looks of aghast and a revolver for a handshake. Nicholas kicked the gun from Hunt's hand, but Norris reached in the desk for another.

"Mr. Norris, please leave the gun in there," Park said in her sweetest voice, but he heeded not her warning. "Honey, did I not ask nicely?"

"You did," mused Nicholas.

Swift as a blink, Park placed a bullet in the hand in which he held the gun, before he could emerge it fully from the drawer. The gun fell back with a loud thud, as he grabbed his hand in pain.

Hunt, however, was not going to take this lying down. He had much more to lose in all this than they did. It took Nicholas only a fraction of a minute to manipulate Hunt into cuffs.

The computer revealed the important information about each child, enabling them to return most of the children to their origin. Sadly, some children were lost forever, because some of the information was either lost or never obtained. It was little consolation, but the criminals received the maximum penalty for the kidnapping of over two hundred children. At last, this mission was over.

Devil's Prey

Park Stevens was no Job, but her time for trial was at hand. Satan had already begun to spin the evils in which he will run to and fro seeking whom he may devour.

It had been two years since Matt's death, and Park had thrown herself into her work, fully. Things were getting to some kind of normal standard again.

Sarah just turned four, and Anna would be two in the fall. She had the curliest strawberry blonde hair imaginable. They both possessed their mother's beauty, but Sarah favored her dad, with dimples as big as canyons. Anna was the spitting image of her mother when she was that age. They were coping as best as they could without Daddy, now.

Uncle Bruce and Aunt Christy took good care of them while Mom was on a job. Sonya was a sister to them both, and things began looking up for them.

Park was not putting her armor on everyday,

according to the Bible, and her spiritual guard was down, allowing Satan to strike when she was not watching.

She was in the process of the girls' nightly routine when the doorbell rang. Flinging them one last kiss goodnight, she fled to answer the call of the bell.

"Park Stevens?" a middle-aged man asked.

"Yes?" She put herself on caution, for a stranger ringing this late at night was unusual.

"Here," he handed her some papers, "you've been served." He left.

Park closed the door, while watching the man rush away. With a curious frown, she opened the envelope containing a subpoena.

A blast from the past in the tune of twenty years slammed her hard. Of all the times for this to happen…well, no time would ever be good for this inconvenience. She startled out of her thoughts at the ringing phone. She knew it was Bruce's nightly call, but tonight, she didn't want to talk to anybody.

"Hello, Bruce."

"Just called to check on you girls." came Bruce's strong voice.

"The girls just went to bed a few minutes ago. They are fine."

Since Matt died, this had been the ritual. Christy or Bruce would call in each night and check on them. Once, Matt told Bruce, that in the event that anything should ever happen to him, he wanted Bruce to take care of them as if they were his own. Bruce didn't need to make Matt this promise, because Park was like a sister to him, and he loved her dearly.

"Good. Remember, you are having dinner with us tomorrow night?"

"Yes, I'll be there after work."

"Okay. Bye," he concluded.

"Bye," she answered.

She returned immediately to her delivery. Why did this have to happen now? She had pointedly cut this chapter from her life over twenty years ago.

"Testify?" She contemplated aloud. There was no way she would ever testify on his behalf. Why couldn't he do this custody thing on his own? Why not leave her dead and buried? The doorbell interrupted her, again. "You are just fooling yourself, if you think I am going to help you," she fussed on the way to the door.

"Were you talking to someone?" asked Bruce upon entering.

"No, I was talking to myself. Didn't I just get through talking to you on the phone? Is something wrong? Is everyone all right?"

"You tell me," inquired the best friend.

"Excuse me?" she quizzed.

"We have been friends for over fifteen years. I know when something is wrong with you. Now, what's up?"

"You came all the way over here, this late at night, because you thought something was wrong with me?"

"I know something's wrong. I hear it in your voice. Now give."

She smiled at him, "You know me too well."

"Well, are you going to tell me or not?'

"I heard from Tim."

"Tim who? Tim... Tim?" He questioningly raised his eyebrows and fell to the couch dumbfounded, "You are kidding me."

"I wish I were."

"How? When? Why?"

"Indirectly, you could say. I received this subpoena," she handed him the legal document. "It seems like brother dear is fighting mommy dearest for custody of his children, and he wants to drag me into it. Can you believe his nerve? What makes him think I would ever help him?"

"I am flabbergasted!" was all he could reply.

"I am supposed to relive the past in front of a court of law. I cannot do this, Bruce. I would rather go to jail for contempt."

"You have no choice. You *will* go to jail if you fail to appear."

"And would that be so bad?" she asked.

"You know I'll be there all the way for you. I

can't make the choice for you, but be sure of your decision before you do anything rash."

"I know you're here for me. I need your prayers more now than ever."

"Honey, you can deal with this. You are strong. You have experience on your side. You know God is with you come what may."

"I'm scared." This simple statement held high impact. "I feel like that little helpless girl again, and I vowed I would never feel that way again."

Bruce knew Park did not scare easily. He had never seen her scared of anything or anyone, save one time years ago. When they were younger, he would chase after her with black snakes and throw them on her, and that didn't even scare her. She took on two girls and a boy in a fight in eighth grade; she got beat up, but she was not scared one bit. There was only one thing he knew had the capability of scaring his best friend.

He stayed the whole night talking, comforting, holding, and remembering with his best friend. This was what friendship is all about. In a way, it was a good thing Matt was not here to see what his beloved was about to face.

Dealing with the Devil

The trial began two Mondays from the subpoena's arrival. The two families decided to make a mini vacation out of it. Considering the circumstances, Sarah and Anna went with Sonya to stay safe at Bruce's childhood home.

Park stayed with her mother's sister, Ava. Over the years, Park maintained a strained relationship with her aunt. Although her mother had disowned Ava years ago for marrying a divorced man and the two siblings had not spoken a word to each other since.

They all left on Friday in order to attend church on Sunday. As usual, this was exactly what they needed. Park sang, *I Must Tell Jesus,* with true conviction. Tears threatened to steal her voice once or twice, but her soul thirsted for the balm of this sanctuary.

It made a big difference for her as she walked into

the den of evil Monday morning. As she and Bruce strode between the two sections of seats, all eyes turned their way, while whispers passed curious lips. Park wanted to turn and run. She made a mistake in coming. She should've stayed home. They could throw her in jail. She was not up to the stares and whispers of strangers.

There her nightmare was, standing before her in the flesh. The horror of his wicked little grin sent chills down her spine. Flashes of torments, caused at his hands, swept into her mind, reminding her of what evil this man was capable.

Fortunately, the bailiff ordered all to stand for the judge's entrance, giving her a reason to avoid him. Consequently, the devil, in the form of a beautiful woman, slithered to the front seat opposite the defendant. The woman was a more mature version of Park and as equally beautiful, but then, the devil comes disguised as an angel of light to deceive whom he will.

Motionless in the back corner of the courtroom

two friends listened to every word. As soon as Park confided to Fred about the late night court order, he promised himself to be there for her. Over the years, Precious had disclosed a small portion of her life to him, and he knew this would be hard on her.

Richardson did not intend to let one of his best agents fly solo through such an ordeal. He knew the potential danger she was in, and came for support. He spoke to the judge privately about her position with the Secret Service and forewarned that his best agent be returned unscathed.

Yet, Park did not see her entourage. She tried to hide from everyone's sight behind Bruce's broad shoulders. The bailiff ordered everyone to sit, and she shrunk to the height of a mere child under her escort's shadow.

To her liking, everyone seemed to forget she even existed as the opposing attorneys argued, whined, and carried on all day. By the time the judge announced they would have to reconvene tomorrow, neither side had accomplished a thing.

Park tried to leave the courtroom with a little dignity, but she could not suppress the shame of her heritage. She had just about decided to opt the jail time and flee before this idiocy sucked her back in, when her eyes caught the devil's. Pure unbridled, straight from the pits of hell, evil shot through her, sending unstoppable chills.

Bruce turned to see what had made her shrink beneath his hand. He, too, watched the poison expound to the point of implosion, an unspoken threat, and finally retreat. He had never experienced anything like that in all his born days. Even Bruce received that message loud and clear.

"Are you going to testify?" he asked as they drove to her aunt's house."

"I seriously considered going to jail, but now, I am telling the truth, the whole truth, and nothing but the truth," she answered determinedly. "I have to think of those children."

After a repeat of the first day, Park caught up with the defense attorney, after everyone left the second day. She demanded to know when she would have to testify, because she had a very important job to return to and did not want to be present for this nonsense if she didn't have to be. In turn, he informed her that she would be the first called after lunch break tomorrow.

The Whole Truth

Park approached the witness box looking deliberately into the eyes of the devil, trying to convey her message. "I am not afraid anymore, I am not that small child, and you cannot hurt me now." Pride had domain where faith should have abounded, thus leaving Park Stevens vulnerable for the devil's work.

"Place your right hand on the Bible. Do you swear to tell the truth, the whole truth, and nothing but the truth, so help you God?" recited the bailiff.

"No sir, I do not swear by heaven or earth, or things in the earth. You do have my word that I shall speak to you the truth. My word is my word."

"You may be seated," the bailiff responded mechanically.

The defense lawyer placed his hands behind his back, paced back and forth for the purpose of intimidation, before finally speaking, "Will you state your name and occupation for the record?"

"Park Stevens, Lieutenant Colonel in the United States Air Force."

"Now, Mrs. Stevens, is this the name you were born with?"

"No," she whispered.

"I'm sorry. Could you speak louder for everyone to hear?"

In an indignant louder tone, "It is not."

"Your honor, I ask that this witness be considered a hostile witness. She and the defendant haven't always seen eye to eye on everything, and I am afraid she will not be forthcoming with all the pertinent information."

"Granted. Get on with it, Mr. Ledbetter," urged the judge. This stupidity had gone on for two days, and after this morning's session, he had already made up his mind.

"What was the name you were born to, Mrs. Stevens?"

She looked for courage from Bruce, who gave it to

147

her with a gentle nod, with his eyes telling her it was going to be all right. "Mary Ann Livingston."

"Would you tell the court the reasons why your name is no longer Mary Ann Livingston?"

"I changed it," she scoffed.

"I understand this, Mrs. Stevens. Explain to this court why you changed it."

"I did not like it, so I changed it," her flippancy infuriated the pompous lawyer.

"You are under oath to tell the truth," demanded the self-righteous attorney.

The plaintiff's attorney jumped up, "Objection, your honor, already asked and answered."

"Sustained; move on Mr. Ledbetter."

"Mrs. Stevens, did you have a happy childhood?"

"What child thinks life is fun?"

He pressed, "Just answer the questions, please. Isn't it true, you spent most of your childhood being thrown from pillar to post?"

"Yes."

"What is it, Mrs. Stevens, that made you feel like

you could not live at home anymore?"

"I guess you could say irreconcilable differences."

"Try saying the truth, Mrs. Stevens," his annoyance began flaring. "What on earth happened, bad enough for a nine-year-old girl to run away, not once, but twice?"

"I would suppose the same things that happens to boys to make them run away," she continued to evade.

"Your honor, I find it difficult to get a straight answer from the witness, so with your permission, I'd like to take a drastic step."

"Council, approach the bench," commanded the judge. Low toned disagreement proceeded for a moment, and then they returned to their former positions.

"Mrs. Stevens, would you please turn around and expose your back?"

"Do I have to, your honor?" she pled with her eyes as well.

"I'm afraid so, Mrs. Stevens. We gave you

opportunity to answer."

Park took one last pleading look at Bruce before turning around, taking off her coat, and slowly unbuttoning her blouse. She pulled the uniformed shirt halfway down her back. She knew what they wanted, and much to the defense attorney's anticipation, the whole room filled with a unison gasp, as her back presented an ugly arrangement of striped scars. She held her head in shame, while the courtroom burst into whispers.

The judge slammed his gavel in vain, "Order in this court!" Regretting his decision to allow this, he stood up, wrapped her coat back around her, and escorted her to his chambers. He had no idea what this would have revealed.

"Here is my restroom, you can repair yourself in there," he told her gently. "I will be here when you get ready."

Park refused to give way to tears. Her humiliation was unbearable. She took as long as she dared to redress and wash her face.

Once again, in the courtroom, she redeemed her character in the judge's eyes, but she could no longer look at Bruce. He had known about the scars from years gone by, but the publicity of it all put it in a completely new level.

She felt the enticement and could not resist the magnetism from the one who brought this shame upon her. At first, she looked at her to hate her, but what she saw in that woman's face, no one would ever believe, had she told it. Her face had a queer contortion, and her eyes bore a black soul hidden within. The woman was no longer beautiful, but horridly possessed within by the subtle one. Then Park could only pity the one whom Satan had desired to possess.

Trial by Fire

Ledbetter continued coldly as if nothing had happened. The smile on his face showed his glee in beating the pride out of this woman. "Mrs. Stevens, what caused those scars on your back?"

"I am not sure I remember exactly."

Well, he thought he had beaten it out of her. Once again becoming agitated, he raised his voice. "Something that horrific and you don't remember? Mrs. Stevens, I thought you were an honest woman." He returned to his table and drew some papers dramatically. Presenting a photograph for her viewing, "Let me refresh your memory, Mrs. Stevens. Is this horse whip what caused those marks?"

She closed her eyes tightly, half way to hold the tears from escaping. How could Tim have brought pictures of this? Her soft voice reflected the onset of a headache. "Yes."

"And at whose hand did you suffer those scars on your back?"

Again, she looked down, unable to respond an audible answer. Her mouth moved in the form of, "Mrs. Livingston," but no sound came forth.

"I'm sorry. I don't believe this court heard your answer. Did you say your mother put those scars on you?"

"I have no mother," Park gritted. For a split second, she forgot her composure. She no longer wished to placate this foolish lawyer.

Once again, the lawyer was pleased with his results, "Mrs. Stevens, answer the question. Is the person that did this to you in the courtroom, today?"

"Yes."

"Would you please, point her out? Let the record show that the witness identified the plaintiff, Abigail Livingston." Park could feel the bullets in her heart from the devil's eyes. "Mrs. Stevens, why did your mother do this to you?"

Park felt all of seven years old again. She dared

not look up, lest she should see anyone looking at her, to find the horrible creature of shame. She had to answer the questions. The judge's stern stare announced that she had beat around the bush long enough. "Because I deserved it."

"How old were you, when you were removed from their custody?"

"I suppose I was about eight or nine."

He pushed harder. "Please tell me, Mrs. Stevens, what could an eight year old child do to deserve such a punishment?"

Sounding like a small child, Park responded in embarrassment. "Once, I snuck and ate some berries out of the garden. Another time, she thought..."

Ledbetter interrupted callously, "You say, 'she', to whom are you referring?"

"Mrs. Livingston."

The lawyer was smiling a sickening grin, "Your mother?"

Park reported louder, "I have no mother."

"I'm sorry. I am confused. Isn't Abigail

Livingston your mother?"

"I have no mother." She repeated adamantly.

"Why are you afraid to call her your mother?" Ledbetter refused to drop this line of questioning.

"I am not afraid. She told me to never call her Mother again, so I do not."

"What did she expect you to call her, then?"

Park shifted nervously. "Mrs. Livingston."

The ruthless lawyer had made the point he wanted to make and changed paces. "Let's get back to the scars on your back. They are the result of more than one beating. Is that correct?"

"Yes."

"Isn't it true, also, that as another form of punishment, your mother would lock you in your room for days at a time, without food or water, or even allowing you to use the bathroom?"

"Yes." The attorney loved her submission.

"Mrs. Stevens, where was your father during all of this?"

"I do not remember. Sometimes he was there. I

assume he was at work most of the time."

"Are you saying that your father allowed your mother to commit these atrocities to you without saying a word?"

"I beg your pardon. I was a failed abortion, no more, no less. That does not constitute someone as a mother or father."

"So you are saying your relationship with your father wasn't a good one?"

"I am saying that I have one Father in heaven. He is all I need."

"I thought surely your father loved you, after the relationship you had with him. Wasn't he compassionate with you?"

Her brow furrowed. She swallowed hard, while trying to remember. "He was rarely there that I recollect. There was no relationship."

"No relationship? That's odd. Mrs. Stevens, your sister testified this morning, in this very courtroom, about your special relationship with your father. Are you denying that you and he were lovers?"

The Unspeakable

"I most certainly do!" she jumped to her feet. She had not been in court that morning, since they were not calling her till after lunch. Park spent the morning with Sarah and Anna. She didn't even know that they had called Lisa to witness in this farce. "I want that stricken from the record. I would…" She grabbed her skull as a pain shot through her temples. What was going on? Had everyone taken full leave of all senses?

The impatient, Mr. Ledbetter spoke loudly, "Mrs. Stevens, I repeat my question again, why would Miss Livingston lie about such a thing?"

Her tremblingly hands held her head. "I am...sure I do not know."

"Shall I read you her testimony?"

"That is not necessary!"

"I quote her words, Mrs. Stevens," he held a transcript of the morning session in his hands, ignoring her pleas to stop, "Mr. Ledbetter: What would you do Miss Livingston, when he would come home before your mother? Miss Livingston: I'd run to Mary Ann and we would run, but we knew he would catch us, so Mary Ann would offer to go. Mr. Ledbetter: What would he do to you if he caught you? Miss Livingston: He... raped us. Mr. Ledbetter: Why would Mary Ann offer to go? Miss Livingston: Because she wanted it, I don't know. Mr. Ledbetter: How do you know what he would do with her? Miss..."

"STOP IT!" She rocked back and forth holding her arms over her ears while tears fled from their ducts. The memories flooded faster than she could bear; his stale cigarette breath, his fingers, his watch. She cried silently, "Please, stop it!"

The judge's gavel banged repeatedly for silence, but Ledbetter ignored the judge's order to, "Shut up!" He wanted to seal this case here and now.

Park was losing consciousness, her head hurt so badly. Everyone's voice resounded as if in a tunnel, and her vision became blurred. Before she could hit the floor, Bruce rushed to her side, lifting her limp body in his arms. The judge directed him to place her on the couch in his chambers, where Bruce nursed her with a cold cloth.

Sitting behind his desk, the judge wasted no time in looking up the facts from yesteryear in the girl's records that the defense had presented for evidence. He had already decided after the girl testified in the morning session that he would not allow the grandparents anywhere near these children. This afternoon's session was supposed to be the simple formalities of conclusion. In all his twenty-two years of serving as a judge, he had never lost control of his courtroom.

As he read the records from two decades ago, he became more disgusted, because he was the judge over this little girl's case, then. It seemed he should remember something this devastating, but somehow he had forgotten. Whoever put these files into the computer, put the basics, so the information was very limited.

Why would he send her back in after knowing these facts? He read the notes on her case. The state assumed responsibility of her because of neglect. Further, he read where she had shown the scars to the social worker, who could not prove where they came from, and dismissed them as evidence. There was no mention of sexual abuse.

The report included a couple incidents with the state appointed fathers on record. It showed no record of an investigation. The social worker concluded that the girl had a creative imagination and made up stories.

He looked to the woman lying on his couch sadly. How could a simple everyday run of the mill custody hearing become so ludicrous? He urged Bruce to carry her to a doctor. This custody hearing was over, and she need not come back here. If he could undo this entire case, he would.

Park refused to go to a doctor. This was not the first migraine she ever had. All she needed was rest.

She walked herself out of the judge's chambers, as a sickening fell upon her weary body and nausea overtook her. Her mind was trying to relocate the memories in that certain spot where they had hidden for all these years.

At her Aunt Ava's house, Bruce tucked Park in bed in a darkened room and retreated to the living room with a heavy heart to wait for the aunt to come. Park never told him about her dad. He knew about everything else, but it appeared that she did not even remember the rest herself until this very day.

He witnessed the courts tossing her from home to home until she was eighteen. Poor little girl, no one ever really wanted her, until he and Matt came along. He never would have dreamed she had survived all that. Her sweet disposition threw him way off on this one. He wished Matt were here, now. It was going to be hard picking up the pieces this time. He was not sure his friend could do it again.

An Awful Ordeal

Park was in a deep sleep, when her aunt left for her second job that evening. Ava worked two jobs to put her daughter through college. Since her divorce, there was no point in spending so much time at home alone, so she enjoyed occupying her time with work.

As usual, Bruce called up to check on her. She almost did not answer the phone. She thought the ringing was a dream, at first, and did not want to stir from her dark rest. Finally, she groggily answered the resounding ring.

During the conversation, Park sensed something was wrong. "Hold on a minute, I thought I heard something," she went to the door and locked it. She briefly looked around the dark house and went back to the phone. "My nerves must be shot, I am paranoid..."

A second later, the phone went dead. Bruce hung up and dialed again; busy. Again, busy. He instructed Christy to keep calling, while he sprinted to his car. Racing like mad, he tore down the highway. It was a good thirty-minute drive to that house, but he made it in less than fifteen. He did not stop long enough to turn the engine off, before running through the open door. The scene before him burned in his mind forever.

Park was in the middle of talking to Bruce, when a long hard object met the back and side of her head, spiraling her into blackness. She felt a sharp pain in her right hand, and now in her left thigh. She was fighting off someone trying to pull at her clothes. This dream seemed so real. She remembered her father's voice of years ago, "You're just like a dog. You keep coming back begging for more. This time, I'll fix you where nobody will ever want you." Another pain ripped through her chest. She could only see blackness.

She couldn't open her eyes. She wanted to wake up from this horrible dream. She tried to roll over, but a pain in her hand stopped her. This was crazy. She was Park Stevens, and she wasn't going to let herself faint like some weakling! She was so cold.

"Okay," she chided to herself, "this is not funny anymore. Get yourself up. Come on." Once more, she tried to turn. Was that Bruce's voice? "Help me Bruce, I can't move." Why would the words not come out of her mouth? "Bruce, here I am. No, Bruce, I don't need an ambulance. When I get up from here, you are going to need one, because I am going to kill you. Help me up. That infernal phone is ringing again. It is going to blow my head up if it rings again. Excuse me friend, but do you mind yapping some other time? I need help up."

"Hold on, Park, help is on the way. Just lay still," Bruce was saying.

She must have chanced upon some sort of wild drug, because she was dreaming some weird stuff. "I wish someone would just blow my head off to make it stop pounding. Oh, there is an awful loud scream. Shut up! My head hurts. Now, I am hearing voices in my head."

Awakening

The next thing Park remembered was opening her eyes in a quiet white room she had never seen before. It hurt to turn her head and see Bruce sitting beside her. Actually, it hurt not to move. The pressure inside her head was intolerable.

Her best friend smiled, "Well, it is about time, Honey." She tried to respond, but the pain was too much. "You gave us quite a scare. They said you are lucky to be alive. Do you hurt much? The doctor said he would give you more pain medicine if you needed it." She tried to raise her hand to her head, but failed. "Lie still. Don't try to move. You rest now." She fell back into the black abyss.

She lingered around in this state for two weeks and three days, before she came to full consciousness. The swelling in her head subsided, and her sight had returned to somewhat normal. It still hurt to move, and her throat was on fire. She deduced that she was in a hospital for some reason, and Bruce was not there.

She lay still in the quiet for hours, before the doctor came in for rounds. He looked into her eyes for the first time. "I see we are awake this morning. How is the patient feeling?" the young doctor inquired.

Park struggled with her sore throat. "What happened?"

He held his finger to his lips. "Rest your throat and get better, then we will talk." He hurried on his way before she could ask more questions.

Bruce gave strict orders to keep mum about what happened. He wanted to be the one to break this news to her. Well, he did not *want* to tell her, but he needed to be the one. By the time the best friend showed up that evening, Park had time to be infuriated at the boycott. She wanted to know what was going on and she meant to find out.

"Some best friend you are," she croaked, "Where have you been? Why did you put me in here? I have to be in court tomorrow."

"Park, Honey, your tomorrow was over two weeks ago," he began gently.

She frowned, "What?"

"You have been in the hospital for seventeen days now."

"Bruce Clayton, are you trying to convince me that I have lost my mind?"

"It is true, Swectie, you have been out cold," insisted her friend.

"What happened?" When he hesitated, she begged, "Please, tell me something. I hurt all over, and I cannot move without pain."

"Park, I can't do this."

"What is it? I have a right to know. Did you wreck me in your car?" her voice squeaked in her agitation.

"No, we are not sure who, but someone walloped

you real good with a sawed off two-by-four."

"Is that why my head hurts so badly?"

"It cracked your skull, causing your brain to swell quite a lot." He paused, trying to muster the courage, "There is more."

"What?"

"Sweetie, he also sexually assaulted you." He stopped there to let her deal with what he just told her. His heart broke, because he was completely helpless as to how to help her. The wild animal look in her eyes actually frightened him.

"I felt it, that is, I think I did. I thought I was dreaming. There was a pain in my hand," she successfully raised her bandaged hand, "and in my leg."

"It is good that you remember. Honey, do you remember who did it?"

"There is something you are not telling me," she accused.

"The pain you felt in your hand and leg was where he pinned you to the floor with knives."

"So, I did not dream it at all? What about the pain in my chest? It hurt the worst."

"That was a knife wound also."

"He stabbed me?"

"Not exactly," he pulled some photographs out of his pocket and held them before her. He watched the tears fill her eyes. He had gutted her from the middle of her breast to her navel. "These are the pictures the police took. Honey, if you know who did this to you, you have to tell us so we can stop him."

"You can't stop him, no one can. Look at me! It is horrible! You should have just let me die. I would have been better off." Coldness filled her eyes. She did her best to turn away from him, demanding him to leave and never come back.

A Friend in Need

Park never knew that Fred and Nicholas witnessed the events of the courtroom that day, or she would have never returned home. Fred asked Nicholas if he wanted to come along, since Richardson had to return after the first day. Neither could have fathomed that before the day was over, they would look at their friend and collaborate in a new kind of awe. Both returned to Charleston with an unspoken vow never to mention to anybody that they were witnesses to such an atrocity.

When Park did not report for work after two days, Richardson investigated the reason why. His anger was unmatched. Park would resent him for interfering; otherwise, he would throw these people under the jail or in the electric chair. As it was, Park was a funny sort. Few agents had wandered past the professional parameters, and warmed his otherwise distant heart, and Park was one of them.

He visited the hospital at odd times, so she would not know he was there. She lay there helpless. How could someone of her caliber let her guard down? He didn't blame her. He was just angry that this had happened to her.

He was overworked and overstressed, when Nicholas caught his growl one day. "Hey Boss, when am I getting my partner back? She has been MIA for a while now."

"She will be a while longer, O'Ryan."

Nicholas sobered from his jovial attitude when Richardson bit his head off, "Is she on vacation?"

"She was in an accident and is recuperating," was the only reply he got.

His heart throbbed to his throat. Accident? When she did not show up, after her court, he had thought she took time off to get her bearings back. He would ask Fred if he knew where she was, so he could check on her.

"Fred, where is Park?"

"I'm sure I don't know this very minute. I haven't

seen her around the last couple of weeks; she might have taken some time off. Why? Having trouble keeping up with that partner of yours? She's a spitfire, that's for sure," laughed the agent friend.

"Richardson said she had been in an accident, I thought you might know."

Hearing this, Fred lost his grin, "What kind of accident?"

"I do not know more than that."

"I wonder why it is hush, hush. You reckon she's on assignment?"

I do not think so," mused Nicholas, "Richardson chewed me out when I asked."

"I'll look into it. If you find anything let me know, and I will do the same."

Nicholas retraced his steps to the last place he had seen her, the courtroom! Had she some kind of breakdown? He closed his eyes right there, "God help her with whatever is wrong with her, I pray, and, if You do not mind, will You help me find her, please?"

Hospitals! If she had an accident, she would be or would have been in a hospital. He called the hospital up in the mountains. The woman responded, "Yes, we had an ambulance call, but no, the patient was so badly hurt, they sent her to another hospital. Yes, we can give you the number."

The bigger hospital did have a Park Stevens admitted on the date two weeks ago, but was transferred to another hospital. The person he question was not sure whether they transferred her to Bowman Gray in Winston Salem, or Chapel Hill, or the one in Charleston, South Carolina. These three were the only ones within driving distance that were properly equipped.

Thinking that maybe they sent her close to home, he tried the local hospital first. They did have her listed as a patient.

Park felt the weight of filth descend upon her wretched soul. She refused to let Bruce visit her anymore. Her body rejected its own skin, making her vomit, even though it threatened to boycott should she move. It became an involuntary reoccurrence, which increased her desire to get out of bed and clean up, which hereby would help to regain her strength.

The doctor wouldn't let her go home until she stopped vomiting. This was strictly policy. The stitches had come out and her wounds were healing up, but the nausea would not go away, and if it were not for this, she could go home.

Park begged for a shower, until they finally granted her one. The wounded leg bucked at the small weight of her bantam figure, so the nurse helped her. "Pull this cord if you have any trouble at all, Mrs. Stevens. I'll be finishing my rounds, but I'll run back, if you need me, okay?"

Park nodded. The water was heaven. Clean at last! The soap lathered with refreshment, the hot water burned the disapproval from her skin.

Prayer for Cleansing

"Excuse me, Miss, but I am looking for Park Stevens' room."

"Yes sir, turn left down that next hall, room 218. I left her in the shower about thirty minutes ago, but she should be out and dressed by now," smiled the nurse at the very handsome man. She noticed he was not wearing a wedding band either.

Nicholas tapped gently on the door of room 218, "Park?" When no answer came, he cautiously entered her room, assuming she was asleep.

She was nowhere in sight, but he heard the water running in the shower and decided to come back later. At the door, he heard soft gasping grunts coming from the other room.

This time, he tapped on the door louder, "Park? It is Nick. Is everything okay?" he spoke strongly. He hesitated. Something was wrong, and she needed help.

"I will be out in a minute." He could hear the secreted sobs under the veil of cheer.

His voice threw Park back into reality; yet, she could not force her brain to accept instruction. The water had turned cold, but she could not stop scrubbing her flesh. The parts of her body that she could reach wore patches, where the scrubbing rasped the skin raw. She reached for the towel, and barely encased it around her frame, when she grabbed the washcloth again. She must wash one more spot.

Nicholas listened to the soft weeping for only a minute. "Park, what in the world are you doing?"

"I can...not get...gasp... the dirt off. I have tried and tried and... sob...it just will not..."

He pushed the door open a few inches. His manly urge was to run to her, pick her up in his arms, and comfort her, until she no longer cried. He deliberately did not concentrate on the mutilation of her body. "But you are clean; there is no dirt on you."

"Can't you see... gasp...the filth? I am covered in

it."

"Come on Partner, your water is cold. Let me help you out of here." He turned the faucets off, pulled the red 'help' cord, and lifted her in his magnificent arms.

By the time he reached her bed, a nurse came in hurriedly. Park kept trying to climb down to return to the bathroom, but he held on tight.

"What do you want?" came an impatient voice from another nurse.

Nicholas's demeanor changed to meet the agitated nurse's attitude. "I need clean towels and clean linens for the bed, immediately."

Nurse Gail did not appreciate his behavior, but she grudgingly fulfilled his bidding. She angrily stomped down the hall to retrieve the linens. "Here, Brenda, you take these to 218. That man didn't sound happy!" She thrust the laundry in Brenda's unsuspecting hands, when she met her in the hall.

Brenda carried her load into room 218 without looking, "Okay, Sweet pea, here you go. Did you miss the bowl?" Upon seeing her patient, she gasped, "Oh good Lord in heaven, child, what happened to you?"

Nicholas took a towel and gently patted Park's face and hair, while Nurse Brenda made a quick job of changing the wet sheets. "Now, you go on out in the hall while I get her dressed?"

"Let me know when you are finished," his strong voice commanded.

The dry hospital gown did little to comfort Park, whose teeth were chattering now. The blanket, on the other hand, basked her in warmth.

The nurse gathered the wet clothing and stepped out to bring in the young man. She took this opportunity to find out what happened.

"Is she going to be all right?" He concerned.

Brenda patted his arm softly, "It is going to take time, but she seems to be a very strong character. I think she'll do just fine."

Back in room 218, Nicholas pulled the chair close to the bed. "Park, I am not sure what is going on with you, but I cannot stand to see you like this." He was stroking her damp hair. "You are one of the strongest people I have ever known. Whatever is going on with you now, you have to pull from that strength."

She barely whispered, "I have no strength," the sobs were only occasional now, "my strength was in the Lord, but even He cannot look at me anymore. I am an abomination that has shamed Him greatly."

"It does not work that way, and you know it. He still loves you, no matter what you do. So whatever is bothering you, lean on His everlasting arms?"

"You don't under...stand."

"Then explain it to me, please. Whatever you did, cannot be that bad. You cannot wash away your sins with water. You know this." Nicholas refused to believe his ideal of womanhood could do anything so abominable."

"He will not wash this away."

"Are you angry with God, then?"

"No, I deserve His wrath. I am being punished."

"What have you done so horrible?"

"I have been...prideful and negligent of His house. I do not honor Him the way I should. He has every right to whip me."

"Park, what happened? Can you tell me?"

"No," a cold hard voice answered. "It is my shame. Please go." She slapped his hand away.

"I do not want to leave you this way."

"Get out! Leave me alone! I hate you!" This was not the voice of his friend.

"You are not getting rid of me that easily."

"Suit yourself, but you will be sorry for getting mixed up with me, you poor stupid man." He began praying diligently for the girl lying in front of him.

His intercession with the Father for the sake of his partner came just in time, for her mind and body were teetering on the edge of insanity and possession. It was into the early streaks of dawn that he lifted his tear stained face toward heaven. The night nurse did not have the heart to disturb him and quietly fled this hallowed place.

Dream Weaver

Park pulled away from Nicholas angrily and closed her eyes tight, until she fell asleep. It took a long time for the blissful blackness to fall on her busy mind. She could call the nurse to give her something to help her sleep, but she wanted to do nothing while *he* was in there.

It was not that easy, though. Once she actually fell into deep rest, it was interrupted by a Man in white, who wandered toward her without seeming to and calling, "Little Mary, why are you so bitter?" His kind face smoothed her burrowed brow, and His gentle voice soothed her soul. "Why are you angry with me, Little Mary?"

"Because You left me alone with Satan, and look at what he did to me," she responded in awe.

"Little Mary," He drew closer, holding His hands to her. She saw holes in them; the right one looked freshly wounded. "Do you really believe, Little

Mary, that you were alone?"

"Father..."

"Yes, Little Mary?"

"You are wounded, Father."

"I was wounded for your transgressions and bruised for your iniquity. Through my stripes, you are healed."

"But Father, I am so filthy. I cannot get clean. The abominations of the heathen are upon my soul. I have partaken of the sins of the fathers. How can You bear to look at me?"

"Little Mary, come unto Me and I will give you rest."

"I cannot ask You to do that for me until I can get rid of this dirty flesh."

"Then ask, Little Mary, and I shall wash you in the Blood and make you white as snow. Have you forgotten My promise?"

"No Father, I cannot ask You to cover so great a sin."

"Sin has no great or small. It is all great." He

spread His arms toward a blood covered cross that suddenly appeared out of nowhere, "Every bit of this, I did for you, Little Mary."

"How can I bear this shame? Look at what he did to me."

"No, Little Mary, look what he did to *us*, for where you go, I go, and what you feel, I feel, for you are Mine and I live in you. You are not alone. You were never alone. If you abide in Me, and My words abide in you, ask what you will, and it shall be done unto you. Without Me, you can do nothing."

"You mean I brought You into this mess? That makes it even worse."

He placed His nail pierced hands on her head. "Little Mary, I am always with you. I will never leave thee nor forsake thee. This is My vow."

"Father, will you wash me? I want you to make me whole again. Will you forgive me for my pride and rebellion?"

"It is already done, Little Mary."

"Father, I am so tired. I don't know if I can go on

anymore."

"You have Sarah and Anna, Little Mary. Do you want to leave them to this life alone? I have given you two strong arms to comfort and rest you. This, have I done because I love you.

Park kept this Spiritual communion treasured in the secret chambers of her heart, too sacred to remember. She opened her eyes, at last, with the Peace of God shining within. The first thing she saw was Nicholas's bent head. However, he was not sleeping. He was still praying. He lifted up anxiously at the realization that she was awake, when she gently touched the dark locks of his beloved head.

"Thank you," was all her course voice allowed.

He kissed her forehead, but the darkness hid the tears that stained his face. Only then was he able to lay his head on her bed and fall asleep.

Seeing her face, Nicholas knew the Comforter had visited his friend. Park's face seemed to glow with joy in the dark. He felt her soft hand in his, which gave him a thrill. Her smooth breaths seemed to lull him into a comfortable sleep. At last, both of them were deep in the slumbers of a natural healthy sleep.

From Whence Cometh My Strength

The doctor was much pleased with her renewed strength. The nurses watched her all day, and she did not get nauseated one time. She progressed enough to sit up in a chair and call her best friend to come visit. She had apologies to make to both her best friends.

Nicholas stayed with her the entire day. He already vowed to himself that he was not going to leave her side unless he had to, so when the doctor made his evening trip, Nicholas remained.

"Park, you gave us quite a scare," began Dr. Bradley, "I will expect no more Brillo baths from you?"

"No sir."

"Good, because I think we are going to let you go home day after tomorrow. The swelling is completely gone in your brain. You should have no more black vision. If you do, let me know ASAP. You were lucky the knife missed your vital organs. If that knife moved a fraction deeper, we probably wouldn't have saved you."

"You did not save me doctor. God did, and there is no such thing as luck." Park informed him.

He continued in annoyance, "Be that as it may, Mrs. Stevens, you are going to need some physical therapy to regain one hundred percent use of your limbs again. The knife severed some of the nerves in your thigh and abdomen. Dr. Horace did a remarkable job in reconnecting them, but you will have limited use of these nerves without the therapy. All the contact information will be in your release papers. Meantime, I want the nurses to get you up six times a day to walk. Don't be frustrated. You will not run any races any time soon. Are there any more questions?"

Park shook her head negatively, but before he reached the door she asked, "Dr. Bradley, what happened to Dr. Douglas?"

"All I know is that he asked me to relieve him as your doctor. Good day Mrs. Stevens," with that came an equally abrupt exit.

Park turned to Nicholas, "I don't think the doctor liked the fact that God deserved all the glory, do you?"

"No, my friend, I do not think he did." He hopped up cheerfully to look out the window. "If you are up to it, we could start that walking tonight?"

"I am game." Park stood up too quickly, to realize the doctor was right. Pain overpowered her leg, and she fell back into the chair.

After helping her to her feet, Nicholas only allowed her three steps. He watched the struggling pain in her face and pushed the chair under her, causing Park to become even more determined.

"I see you are anxious to get out of my care," said Nurse Brenda upon entering.

"We have to start somewhere, why not here and now?" Nicholas offered.

The nurse thought the young man was especially

charming tonight. His voice sounded youthful, and the lines of worry had miraculously disappeared. His green eyes sparkled with delight.

The patient had a charm about her now. She could see Park's natural features now that the bruises were healing. She had spent hours brushing this patient's bountiful hair, thinking how dreadful it was they had to shave that gap for the stitches.

"How did you do, Mrs. Stevens?"

"Please, call me Park. You have seen me at my worst, you are entitled," laughed the patient.

Nicholas informed, "Three steps."

"Wonderful!" exclaimed the nurse.

"What is wonderful about it," argued Park, "Three paltry steps, I am like a child."

"That's a perfectly natural reaction for what you are going through. In time, they will heal, and you will learn to use those muscles and be back to your normal self. Now, here are some hand exercises I want you to do. Probably the hardest part of it all is the coordination you must use with both hands. Here

189

try this." Nurse Brenda showed her what to do.

"Will she be sore after her workouts?" asked Nicholas.

"Usually, but there's a hot tub down on the ground floor, in the rehab section, that she can soak in. We'll go down after our walk tomorrow, but if you want to use it before then, just say the word."

"Thanks," Park smiled.

Nurse Brenda left the two alone once more to attend to the other patients.

Park pondered aloud, "Nick, I have been thinking, you can't keep babying me this way. You have your own life to live. You have other people in need of your kindness and help, maybe a girlfriend. I appreciate your devotion, but I have to recuperate, and if you don't let me do for myself, I'll never be whole again."

The words cut deeper than the wounds on his partner. He would run through fire for Park, and she was rejecting him. Woe his broken spirit, and his voice sad, "I guess you are right. I will let you do

190

this on your own. Richardson wants to send me out in the field for a couple months span; I guess I could go."

"Now, why are you allowing me to prevent you from doing your job? It will get us both in hot water with boss if you hang around me."

"I understand. I order you to be home and healed when I get back, you hear?" His fit frame had a droop, when he reluctantly turned to leave.

"I will," she saddened because he was leaving so easily, "Nick, I will never forget your prayers for me."

An Awkward Proposal

When she arrived home, a small bouquet of daisies greeted her at the front door. She could not escape the charmed smile that claimed her lips. Once more, the mystery resurfaced. Ever since the key to the paradise in Montana appeared after Matt died, occasion would bring her most beloved blossoms and drop them in her lap. If she could find the owner of the hideaway, she would find the flower bearer.

She was like the daisy flower in the manner that they were both simplistically lovely to look upon, they both were a wild life and both independent. When they were in full bloom, Park loved to take Sarah and Anna out to the fields and make crowns for their golden hair out of the daisies. Sarah showed Anna the secret to connecting them, and they made necklaces, bracelets, and rings to match. They loved to pick them for their mother as a surprise.

Somehow, someone knew about her passion for

these beauties and showered her with all the colors from time to time. She suspected Christy might be the flower fairy, but if she was, the fairy never gave a clue to her secret.

Sarah and Anna thought they were in Heaven, spending all this time with Mommy. They thrilled in nursing her day after day. It was a rare opportunity for her to be home so long at one time.

Bruce and Christy found out that Sonya was going to be a big sister, which gave Christy a good excuse to take a leave from her job and became a fixture around the Steven's house. It pleased her much to explore a new kinship. She gained the opportunity to learn why her husband loved this friend so much.

At first, Christy assisted Park in everything, but as her strength returned, Park became insistent on doing more on her own. The invalid was determined not to depend on anyone for any reason, vowing to depend only on God.

Rehabilitation proved a very difficult deed, but Park resolved to get back to the force as soon as physically possible. Her fortitude drove the ones around her further away, though. She held her faith strong in the Lord, depending on Him, but becoming independent of all fleshy support, she wanted to accomplish full recovery without the aid of her friends.

Something sad changed in Park Steven's tormented soul. Once again, she learned clearly that man could and would let her down. There are times when only God could help. God would always take care of His servant, just as He did for Daniel in the den of lions, when all seemed impossible. While her friends looked upon this change as a pity, she looked upon it as a drawing to the Holy Spirit.

Seven weeks of torturing rehab ensued. Park enlisted Spirit in her daily workout to retrain her legs in manipulative skills. In addition, practicing the piano worked wonders for her hands, but as in all things, she exercised to the extreme in order to be one hundred percent at a quicker rate.

She had not heard from Nicholas since that night

in the hospital, and with so much time on her hands, she thought about him often. Because he had left her so easily without an argument, she realized how much she had imposed on his kindness, and regretted having kept him for so long in her selfish need. She missed his friendship and confidence. For over two years, this duo team had shared with each other things that they could tell no one else.

She began to leave the rehab center with a dull heart, when a familiar face crossed her path. "Excuse me, I don't mean to be forward, but do you remember me?"

Park looked coldly into the prettiest brown eyes she had ever seen, and her tone grew indifferent, "I know exactly who you are, Dr. Douglas."

"You are angry. I was hoping you wouldn't be," he put his hand on the door to open it for her, "I was wondering if you would like to have a cup of coffee with me?"

"I do not think I would care to go anywhere with you; if you will excuse me." she reached clumsily for

195

the door herself, but his hand remained.

"I will accept that under one condition. You tell me why you are angry."

"I owe you no explanation. You are not my doctor and have no right to 'condition' me for anything," she said with finality.

He laughed, "I thought so. You are angry because I asked Dr. Bradley to replace me as your doctor?"

"Do you know what it feels like to find out you are so hideous to look upon, your own doctor can not even stand to look at you? You are relieved of your duty, doctor. Now, if you will excuse me." This time she pulled the door open and stepped into the cool autumn air.

He followed her slow practiced steps. "Mrs. Stevens, I can fully explain. It is not what you think. Please, may I have that opportunity?"

She eyed him warily. His honest face licensed her to answer, "One cup of coffee, and that is all. I will give you no more time than that."

"Are you driving yet?" He asked.

"No, I am taking a taxi."

"We can take mine." He opened the door to a BMW parked on the side of the road. He drove up the coast a little way to a small cafe he loved to frequent.

Once seated at a booth in a secluded corner, away from the staring truck drivers, he began, "Now, may I explain why I resigned as your doctor?"

"Go ahead," she simplified. Turning to the waitress, "Water, please."

"Coffee," he waited for the waitress to leave. "You have not figured it out yet?"

"You speak in riddles Doctor, what do you mean?"

"I was on duty the night they brought you down. I spoke to your friend that accompanied you, when you came, because I needed some papers signed by the next of kin, and I assumed he was your husband. He told me your husband passed a couple years ago." He held his head, as if admitting to an indiscretion. "Be assured, you were and are not hideous to look at.

I didn't want a doctor/patient relationship with you. There was something in your eyes, when you opened them and looked at me...do you know how beautiful you are?" He searched her face for some response. "I would like to get to know all about you, your favorite food, flowers, or how you spend your time. Would you consider giving me that opportunity?

The doctor was very good looking with his blond hair and perfect smile, but Park was not interested in beginning any kind of relationship. It was almost three years since she lost her beloved Matt, but during the lonely nights, it seemed as if it had only been a few days.

He continued gently, "I'm off Wednesday. We could have a quiet dinner, if that would be convenient for you?"

The Doctor and Mrs. Stevens

In order to stay grounded in her Solace and to continue to heal completely, she made several day trips to the mountains in order to attend her favorite church. The emotional scars lay buried deep beneath the surface, but with God's help, they were subsiding.

On the other hand, the physical scars took a little longer. Paul mentioned that he knew a plastic surgeon that would be able to graft most of them away, but Park kindly refused. She was not so vain as to worry about appearance. More importantly, she never wanted to forget these, her battle scars. They would keep her humble before her Master.

As the days turned into weeks and the weeks into months, she worked hard, until she was ready to get back into the swing of things.

Quite a few weeks passed, before she saw any sign of her partner. Even then, she hardly saw him at all. He always seemed too busy to talk. Richardson gave him his own office, and Park felt forbidden to enter his domain. She troubled herself many times about the distance that had wedged its way between them.

She agreed to spend some time with the young doctor; however, it seemed to be going faster than Park wanted. Paul determined from the first day that he wanted a future with her, but Park did not desire to be in a serious relationship. She did not even want to consider dating. Friendship is all she wanted from any man.

Doctor Douglas requested her presence at a gala event, a ball for charity, where each plate cost $500.00, which went to the research of POWs. Because this was such a worthy cause, Park agreed.

Naturally, Paul included Bruce and Christy in the invitation, but they declined since the mother-to-be was so far along. However, she helped paint Sarah and Sonya's face and attire them in their frilly gowns. In their hair, each one wore one of the white roses out of the twelve dozen Paul sent to Park earlier that day.

They teased Anna and pranced around twirling the

frill on their dresses making the little sister drift upstairs to find comfort in her mother.

Park placed her hand on Anna's hair. "Did you know that you have your Daddy's smile?" The strawberry blonde curls bounced. Park pushed her little lips into a smile. "Will you let me see your Daddy's smile?" Anna's lips fell back into a pout. "Do you want to tell Mommy why you are sad?"

"Why can't I be biggur than Tharah?"

The mother smiled, "You are just the perfect size, little one." She lifted the little girl to her hip. Her little legs reached around Park's waist. "If you were any bigger, you would not be able to snuggle in your special spot. I tell you what," she placed Anna on the bed, went to her jewelry box, and pulled out a gold chain with a gold band dangling from it. "This is your Daddy's special ring. I need an equally special young lady to take care of it for me tonight. Sarah is too old, and I was wondering if you would be my little helper tonight and wear it for me?"

Matt's smile appeared on her little face. "Fank oo,

Mommy."

Park slipped into the gown she had used on the baby selling assignment, and prepared to slip into her elbow length gloves. She held the small clear baggie containing her rings in her palm, pondering in her sadness, when Anna came upon her. The hospital had taken her wedding rings off for her surgeries and returned them in the baggie. She had never taken them off before. She could not replace them on her fingers. Matt had put them on the first time, and he would have to be the one to do it again, so she had no rings on her finger, any more.

Suddenly, she felt guilty. She shouldn't be happy without Matt. She gathered her little girl in her arms and proceeded toward the stairs. She didn't feel like going, but she had already committed.

She ascended the stairs as a picture of perfect splendor. The new hair from where the doctor had shaved it for the surgery had grown out about three inches, and she had pulled it all back to cover the spot so that no one would be able to tell.

Paul sent a limousine to chariot them to the affair, because he had to work late. He sent word that he would meet them at the benefit. The fancy vehicle enthralled the girls with all its knobs, buttons, TV, lights, and everything.

The dashing doctor awaited them at the benefit. Sarah and Sonya pretended they were royalty, while Anna clutched one tiny palm around her daddy's wedding band and the other around her mother's hand.

Taking one look at Park, Paul exclaimed, "You look incredible!"

Park smiled her thanks and kept her hand in his arm to announce her partnership with him. She kept fidgeting her slender fingers around Anna's little one nervously.

Mingled laughter pleasantly lingered throughout the great hall during the meal. A string band played soft music, while certain couples danced to the rhythm. Paul tried to persuade his date to dance with him, but she pleaded inability.

A New Alliance

"I want you to meet someone I think you will like." He spotted the chairman and led her in his direction. "Grant, I would like you to meet Park Stevens. Park, this is the chairman of this benefit, my good friend, Grant Grayson. He has spent years fighting for our POWs."

Park flashed her charming smile, "I am pleased to make your acquaintance." She gave a slight curtsey. "I would like to learn more about this cause." She cast her magic spell upon him.

"I will be glad to discuss this cause whenever and wherever, especially with such a charming lady. Are you seriously interested, or just being nice?"

"I do not *play* nice. Is there any way I can assist?"

"Where did you find such a charming young lady, Paul?"

"Mr. Grayson, what made you interested in this POW rescuing?"

"Please, call me Grant. May I call you Park?" She nodded, and he continued sadly. "My son joined up six weeks after his eighteenth birthday. He served his two years and was about to come home. Four days before his release, his plane went down, and he has been MIA ever since."

"Do you think he is alive?" Park was earnest in her quest for information.

Paul had explained that she was semi-retired from the Air Force, and Grayson stood in awe. He assumed she was just a secretary or something, but her converse revealed experience.

"There is only a slight chance," Grant replied sadly.

"Then, what are you doing about it?" she queried.

"Trying to get enough funding to buy back all the prisoners we can find."

"How long have you been trying this approach?"

He saddened his expression, "I have been trying to get some sort of structure ever since they told me my boy was MIA. For the last three years, we have held these benefits to raise the money. It feels like when we take two steps forward, we are thrown back three, because they keep changing the price or the conditions."

Park thought for a moment, "Have you considered any alternatives?"

"Such as?"

"Has it been confirmed the POWs are, indeed, there?" She was forming an idea.

"Not in so many words, but they are there. I know it."

A couple interrupted them at this point, sweeping Grant Grayson into another conversation, while giving Park time to contemplate these thoughts. She promptly excused herself to the restroom to pray to her Guide.

Throughout the entire evening, Mr. Grayson explained in detail about his mission. As the party drew to a close and guests were exiting, Paul suggested they leave, but Park requested staying a few minutes more. As the crowd dwindled down to a few, Park took leave of her date in search of Mr. Grayson.

"Mr. Grayson, this is for you. However, I just have one string." She subtly slipped a paper in his hand, which he slyly opened. It was a personal check for a hundred thousand dollars! Tears filled his eyes, and he could not stop the embrace of appreciation within him. "You see, my husband was a prisoner of war and brutally killed as one. It is my desire to help restore our men."

His voice cracked slightly, "You said a string was attached?"

"You are not to use it for buying your son back," she glanced cautiously around. "I want you to select a team of soldiers, who served with your son. I am recovering from an accident, but when I am back on top, we are going to get that team in and bring them back ourselves. There will be no buying."

Gant looked doubtful, "I don't think it's possible."

"I have access to some incredible resources."

A dawning hope came into his eyes, "You really

think we can pull this off?"

"I do. I need you to research their whereabouts to present an accurate and thorough location, exactly how much opposition will we face, what kind of security, ingress and egress points, every little detail. Take this money to buy anything we need."

"I know some men, who served with Shawn the first year of service, that will help." He dared to imagine this plan might work. Since his son's disappearance, his entire life had built up to this one great climax, and it might finally have come.

"We will need two that are capable of flying. Depending on the surrounding circumstances you uncover, we can determine how few ground men we can get by with."

"I will get on it Monday morning, first thing. Do you have a timeline in mind?"

"Can you give me three months? That will give us more time to find out all there is to know about this before we go in."

"I can hardly wait!" he cried.

The Request

"I hope you had a wonderful time tonight," Paul looked across the front seat of his car at the sleeping girls. "Grant really liked you a lot. I don't think I have ever seen him that enchanted by anyone before."

"I believe we all had a great time," she followed his gaze to the back seat. "Thank you for inviting us."

He grinned with pleasure. "Tuesday is Christmas. I was wondering… Would you and the girls… I would like you to meet my family. My mother will just adore you. I am planning to leave in the morning and stay all week, and I want you and the girls to accompany me."

Park could not help smiling at his nervousness. "Paul, that sounds nice, and if I did not have prior plans, I might take you up on that offer. Matt and I rather have a tradition to spend Christmas with our friends. It is already planned."

The doctor was disheartened. He wanted his parents' blessing on his choice for a bride. He had not counted on her rejecting the invitation. In his disappointment, he said very little the remainder of the ride.

The two silently carried the three sleeping children up the stairs and put them in bed. A quick pang pierced her heart, as she reached down to kiss Anna's head. How could she betray her beloved Matt this way? The conversation with Grant Grayson and Anna's reflection of Matt reopened the wounds of losing her sweetheart, and the guilt of being with someone else crept in.

Back in the den, she lit a fire in the fireplace, and her guest joined her on the sofa. They sat in the dark watching the flames flicker and dance around the room, he in his disappointment and she in her mourning.

"Paul, I hope you are not too disappointed. Perhaps we can go another time."

"I just wanted to show you off. I wanted to show my family how very special you are." He leaned toward her with a longing desire to ask her here and now to be his wife. "I have your present, and since I am leaving tomorrow, I want to give it to you now." He reached in his pocket.

Park opened the box that held a diamond pendant heart embedded in sapphires. She gasped, "Paul, it is exquisite!"

"And yet, does not compare to you." He kissed her head. "Here, let me put it on you."

Her tiny neck displayed the jeweled heart flawlessly. "You should not have done this." She toyed with the expensive gift nervously. "I do not deserve something so extravagant, besides I have nowhere to wear such a piece. Please, don't make me responsible for this fortune."

"My love, you deserve so much more than I can give. You take it, wear it, and think of me when you do. It could never know a more perfect home than where it is right now."

Park hesitantly retrieved her gift for him from under the tree. How could she give him these silly season tickets to the opera after his expensive present? "This seems so inadequate compared to this necklace."

The look of joy on his face spoke volumes, "Now, we can go for a whole season together without fighting the crowds. Darling, this is just wonderful. Thank you."

As they sat entranced by the firelight, Paul decided that he was going to propose when he returned. He was not a fool to wait around. He would ask Park Stevens to be his wife.

A Lonely Christmas

The day Nicholas O'Ryan walked out of that hospital room dejected and miserable, his heart fell. The enchanted spell was broken. She had dismissed him. She had not wanted him at all. He enjoyed helping her. He thrived on her needing him.

When he returned from that long assignment, and found out she was dating the doctor, his happiness ceased to exist. For the very first time he admitted, if only in prayer, what he never dared even think before.

"Oh God in Heaven," he cried, "I love her! I love her whereas I never thought I could love anyone, but she does not love me. She chose another. Oh God, help me to stop loving what I can never have."

He couldn't be near her. Her pleasant scent was like a fresh summer day, the softness of her curls between his fingers or against his face, the intensity of her beautiful eyes that pierced his guilty soul would give away his secret. When she was close, he could not stop his heart from betraying his love.

He watched her from a distance, longing to be near, but daring not the risk. Now she was expecting him to spend Christmas with her family as usual, as if nothing has changed, with that man there! She had sent him a note of invitation, but he had not given her any response. He was hoping to escape the awkward event if possible.

When Park had heard nothing from Nicholas Monday evening, she called upon Fred to intervene. The rumor was, he informed her, that Richardson sent him on assignment until after Christmas.

Bruce and Christy came over that night to exchange their gifts early. There had been a change in plans at the last moment. Bruce's mother had been ill for some time. It appeared that this might be her last Christmas, and he needed to be with his precious momma. They agreed to let Sonya spend Christmas with Sarah and Anna. Bruce did not particularly want her to see her grandmother in this condition.

With this turn of events, she wondered if maybe she should have accepted the invitation from Paul. No, Fred would be there, and he was family, so no, she made the right choice.

With only a few hours of sleep, Mrs. Stevens rose early, so that delicious smells wafted through the open window and hit Fred full in the face before he ever rang the bell.

Sonya opened the door. "Uncle Fred, come on in. Sarah and I are making the cookies. Would you be our sampler?"

"Why, I believe I would enjoy that. Lead me to them," he laughed as she pulled him to the kitchen.

They spent the day eating, opening gifts, playing and singing songs. They made a trip to the horses to give them their presents of apples and sugar cubes. The girls pulled Fred here and there, but he didn't mind. He grinned as if he was sixteen again.

Occasionally, Park passed a sad expression of desertion quickly over her sweet face, which caused the old man to remark, "Precious, he has to work.

You know how it is. How many holidays have you missed for work?"

She shared a sad smile, "I was not even thinking of Nick. I know he has to work. It is a shame that he had to miss out on this delicious dinner."

"You outdid yourself this year. That was the best pumpkin pie I ever ate."

"You old softie, you would say that if it tasted like mud." She kissed his rugged cheek. "Come on girls. It is bath time. It is getting very late."

"Ah Mom," Sarah complained.

"Already!" Sonya seconded as Park marched them up to gather their laundry.

She laid out their clean pajamas and started down the steps with a load of clothes. "Precious, come here a minute," Fred called from the kitchen.

"I will be there is just a minute." She dropped the load in the laundry room, before starting into the kitchen.

Fred leaned on the frame of the doorway, "Someone is here to see you."

216

The Unexpected Guest

She entered the kitchen to greet the schoolboy grin of her partner. "I am starved!" he exclaimed.

Nicholas requested this work assignment, thinking he would have a good excuse not to have to come to the dreaded dinner. He had made up his mind not to impose while the doctor was there, but the magnetic force was mightier than he was, so he worked overtime to finish early. It was worth risking all that to see the glorious expression on the face of his never-to-be lover, at that moment.

Her smile could not hide her exhilaration. "Nicholas, I am so glad you made it."

Park flew to setting the table with the bounty of the day. After their encounter at the hospital, she didn't want to appear too anxious to see him.

Nicholas was still enjoying his meal when three wet bedraggled girls screamed excitedly, for Uncle Nick had come at last. They didn't even let him finish his pie before dragging him to the tree, forcing a present into his hand, and demanding he open it.

His gift from them was some crude pictures they took with Sarah's camera. One picture of Sonya, Sarah, Anna, and Mom was special enough that they framed it and gave a copy to Fred, Bruce, Nicholas, and Paul.

Nicholas looked into the immortalized blue that stared at him from the paper. "God, she is beautiful. Please take away this love that will never be returned," he prayed. So virtuous were those eyes that seemed to look through to his soul, and she hated him. She had told him she hated him. He loved her, and she hated him. How his heart tormented!

Fred went up to read the girls a story for bed, when Park handed Nicholas a box wrapped in silk. The woman's fancy touch made opening the gift awkward under his large fingers.

Nicholas gently caressed his leather bound Bible, that lay inside the silk wrap. On the first page, she wrote in her delicate hand, *May you never forget*

what it stands for, or how it is given in the love of
Christ to my dear friend. This was the most treasured
gift anyone had ever given him.

When she opened the box he handed her, her hand
flew to her mouth, while she fought hard to keep the
tear faucets turned off.

Nicholas had delved into Matt's death, and in
doing so, he found out that the hero had never
received a medal for his last service to his country.
Someone had dropped the ball and grossly neglected
giving his family his Purple Heart. Nicholas called in
several favors in order to acquire the medal to present
to the beloved widow.

The bricks, which had formed a wall between
these two, began to crumble. Nicholas realized that it
was more important to have his friend and
trustworthy partner, than a lover who would never be.

He would not let these foolish notions interfere
and keep him from his duty as friend. He could
never tell her of his true heart; so how would she
know? He couldn't blame her for not loving him.

The Plan

Dr. Bradley gave the green light for full status return. This was music to Richardson's ears, because he had assignments waiting for the dynamic team to stop the criminal schemes. Together again, this duo reminded Richardson what a lethal combination this was.

Park had not forgotten Grant Grayson's rescue mission. She and Richardson discussed it in depth several times, but his position with the government would not allow him to conflict his loyalties. He could not advise or actually endorse the usage of government property; however, he unofficially approved of any resources she might need out of respect for Park and this cause. He wanted to help her openly, but the government maintained that there were no more POWs.

Kincaid was more open about his involvement. He did not send any announcement out or anything, but he was a sounding board for the team. He was able to conquer information that no one else was able to obtain.

Time was nearing for execution. Grayson picked three men and another woman that had served time with Shawn. He also acquired and serviced two retired military helicopters for this rescue, so the plans were coming together.

The first member he chose was Duncan, the only woman in Shawn's platoon. She was an excellent pilot. She was supposed to be with the rest of the platoon, but broke her arm on the training session and could not go on the fated operation.

Creasman was the explosives expert. During his service, he blew up bridges before the enemy could cross. He was a solidly built biker, with tattoos completely covering his arms. He said little and scowled a lot while rubbing his bald head. His hearing lacked, because the explosions had damaged his inner ear. He served with Shawn during his first year.

Staton was the third picked. He was a wiry fellow who had wiled his way in and out of the nemesis's snares, which earned him the nickname, 'Weasel'. There had been huge publicity about a sneak attack he had made for his country, which earned him an accommodation. He had kinky red hair that he shaved for the time being. His connection was not with Shawn. He had served with Creasman, who recommended him.

Shipman was the final choice and the second pilot. He had two brothers killed in war and the third brother was with Shawn when their plane went down. He wore his brown hair in the fashion of a mop top. His kind eyes were always watching everything at once.

Each one chosen was the best for this job because of their skills, and they had heart for wanting to succeed in this quest.

The only fall back was that word spread that Creasman had problems with an outsider trying to come in and take charge. His dislike for Park manifested to everyone involved. Just because she had a little money to throw away, did not validate her participation.

Park included Nicholas in on the comments Creasman had made to the others, and for this reason requested he watch her back. He agreed that he didn't trust this Creasman either. He even suggested replacing the brute, but Park insisted he was a crucial member of the team. The preparations were near completion, and it was too late to start over with someone else.

They agreed. No one else was to know that Nicholas was shadowing the crew, save Kincaid and Grayson. That way, Park could remain safe.

In between assignments, Park joined the crew for the training and run-throughs, so that when execution day came, everything would run smoothly. During this training, the other three-team members came to know and like the outsider. She impressed them with her agility, accuracy, and ability. At first, they thought she was terribly young to be of much account, but she proved to work hard for the same cause.

They realized that working together meant saving lives, and they must put their complete trust in each other if this mission was going to work. Creasman trusted his old platoon, because they had been tested and tried, but he was not going to depend on some little girl, who would blow away in a strong wind. He barely tolerated Staton.

Ferreting Out The Enemy

Shipman and Duncan remained in the city until time to fly in for egress, while the rest of the crew spent twenty-eight hours crawling into the prison camp. Finally, they were able to spy the activities below. They watched until dark.

Weasel used the cover of darkness to infiltrate one of the prison cells. Being on the inside enabled him information otherwise unobtainable. When the morning broke and the guards came to take the prisoners to work, they did not realize he had taken the place of a very weak prisoner.

There were two men in the cell. Both were weak, thin, and bald and were hardly able to speak. He swapped clothes with the one that had a nasty cough, leaving him to hide under his bunk all day, while he scoped out the surroundings.

True to his reputation, Weasel remained undetected. When darkness fell again, he returned to the others with enough information to accomplish success.

"There are only the six prisoners," he explained. "There are two men in each..." the sound of whirring propellers drowned his voice.

The team took cover while a chopper flew down to the camp. Several men unloaded. Half an hour later, several loaded before the chopper ascended out of sight. No one dared breathe for the entirety of this time.

Weasel continued to explain, "They must be changing shifts. They come twice a week to relieve the others. There are two men at all times in the guard tower. They live there twenty-four seven, alternating hours. Seven guards escort them to work. The boss never leaves. He is the key. We need to get him first because he stays next to the radio. Ten more guard the camp at all times, five during the day, and five at night. They have sleeping barracks behind the prison."

"How much fire power do they have?" asked

Grayson.

"They stock quite a bit of back up in a building at the end of the barracks. If anyone tries to destroy it, it will automatically take the prisoners with it. It will be impossible to blow it up."

Everyone looked to Grayson for instruction. The ammunitions shed caused a contingency. The object still was not to kill, but just rescue their own. Twenty to four was not good odds.

The Execution

Creasman and Weasel slipped out after darkness fell and secured the explosives for the tower and radio shed. The plan was in motion. As soon as the guards swapped out in the morning, they were to detonate the explosives and prevent the munitions shed from exploding, if possible.

Grayson gave the signal at the appointed time. When the two bombs exploded systematically, Grant and Park raced to their positions. Retrieval began abruptly, while the air filled with sounds of war.

They found five men in the barracks, one of whom was too weak to walk. Grayson placed his son upon his shoulders and carried his limp frame to safety. Park shouted in the native tongue, asking where the last prisoner was.

As expected, the guard would not reveal, but the prisoner closest to her pointed to another hut. "He's sick!"

Park and Grant ran across the yard with their precious cargo, when the impact of the munitions shed blowing up threw them all in the air. They could hear their rescue in the air. They must hurry.

Park left the POWs with Grayson at the rendezvous point and sprinted to the hut on the other side. She shot through the hut with the intentions of saving the last one.

Creasman shadowed her. When the temptation crossed his path, he raised his gun to her back as she bent and lifted the sick soldier on her back. He contemplated pulling the trigger, but Something refused him the pleasure.

As she turned to face him, the soldier, whose life was nearly gone, looked confusedly into Creasman's eyes.

None had time to ponder what had just happened, because something was wrong. Duncan was not landing. There seemed to be more air sounds than should be, and then an explosion ignited mid-air. Duncan landed abruptly.

They put the last POW in Shipman's helicopter. They were ready to fly, when Duncan shouted to Park.

Park ran to her, "I have been hit. She'll not fly! Load up in the other one, quick!"

"Go on, get in it," she returned, "I will see what I can do here."

Duncan argued, "I'll stay and help."

"I am going to fix her to blow if they try and take her up. Here help me get this grenade under the rudder. If she blows, I want her to take as many as she can."

Duncan ceased firing at the coming enemy, when Park had it complete. Creasman, who had followed the stupid little girl again, covered their return to the working escape vehicle.

Shipman was waiting on Creasman to take off, but he went down on the last stretch. Without a thought, Park jumped to the rescue. He was too heavy for her to carry, so she crutched him to the plane, while Weasel fired at the enemy.

Once Creasman was in, Park motioned for Shipman to fly on. The overloaded chopper teetered under the weight.

With the realization that Park was going to remain in enemy territory alone in order for them to escape, Weasel jumped over Creasman to the ground at the last minute. He grabbed Park's hand, as the two ran for the cover of tall grass.

The two prepared themselves for anything, for they were in unknown hostile land with the savage natives on their heels. There was a waterfall opening into a vast river a couple miles east, which became their destination. Tracking would be difficult if they could reach the falls.

They ducked for cover when they heard the dreaded wings coming near them. Looking for an escape, Park saw the glorious sight of *Dixie's Pride*. To show how God watches over those who are His, He had sent dear Nicholas to the rescue.

"It is okay, she is friendly! Come on!" Park shouted and began running again in the opposite direction of the enemy.

Nicholas found his target and searched for something long to push out the rope ladder. Steadying her up, he flew in the direction of his cherished damsel. Good, she was still running.

She insisted Weasel mount first, but he refused. "Then, we go together," she yelled, and they both grabbed the blessed rope ladder.

Nicholas ensured their safety before taking leave. The two rescuers made it to the top and struggled into the fleeting chopper.

Park was so relieved that her partner bailed her out again, that she graced him with a kiss of appreciation on his dark head. "You have pulled me out twice now. I am indebted to you for life."

"We got them all!" Weasel breathed happily. The action exhilarated him.

"Nicholas, this is Staton, I could not have survived without him."

"Then I am the one indebted, pleased to make your acquaintance," smiled Nicholas.

"Ah, she's just saying that, I didn't do much," he responded modestly.

They stopped at the reunion site long enough to release Weasel and refuel, before heading home. Park couldn't afford any notoriety that this rescue might bring. It might jeopardize her work. She was just grateful to be going home.

Friendships

Paul thrilled at Park's return. She had not told him where she was going, again. Actually, all her disappearing acts were beginning to annoy the doctor. She was constantly vanishing for long periods without any explanation.

When she made him promise never to speak to her, if he saw her in public, he became distrustful. Why did he have to pretend not to know her? To further his aggravation, she wouldn't give him a straight answer, whenever he questioned her about her job. She told him she was retired from the Air Force, so then why did she keep leaving on business?

Could she possibly be unfaithful to him? Could she really betray him this way? No, he knew she was not the kind of person that would cheat. He was just so frustrated about her secrecy. Why else would she keep him in the dark?

Maybe it was that Nick character. She did seem to

spend an awfully lot of time with him. From what he could perceive, Nick had affections for the woman he intended to marry. Maybe Park did not return Nick's attraction, and he was trying to seduce her. That must be it. Park wouldn't cheat on him.

He decided to become closer and more attentive to his lover, and then Nick would bow out of the picture. Maybe he could ally with Bruce and Christy to find out what he could about that Nick guy, but when his schedule prevented him from spending as much time as he desired with her, he considered accepting the offer of partnership in a prominent office.

If he took this partnership, it would enable him to make the official move and propose, before he lost this jewel. However good the plan sounded, Paul Douglas went to the extreme, as usual. In an attempt to prove he could take care of Park the way she deserved, he showered her with expensive gifts, until she demanded he stop.

It was not that Park was not fond of this handsome

blond doctor, quite the contrary; she had come out of her shell with him. Although she was not ready for marriage, she enjoyed spending time with him, thoroughly. Other than squandering good money on useless trinkets, he said and did all the right things. Paul admitted he had not been the kind of Christian he knew to be, but he was saved. That was all Park needed to know, besides the fact that Sarah and Anna loved him also.

Since summer had arrived in full array, the cookouts and friendly get-togethers were frequent. Park made sure to include the doctor in all the events, much to the insistence of three little girls.

Paul fell to the background, when Matthew Parker Clayton arrived with shouts of acclamation. In Park's opinion, he was the prettiest baby boy ever born. Mr. and Mrs. Clayton were ecstatic over his arrival.

As Park looked out over the vast ocean with the smell of newborn babe tickling her nose from her porch, she realized she was blessed with friends and loved ones in harmony and one accord. This new little life in her arms brought so much joy.

Bruce watched Park from his chair. She had healed so well. He knew little of what happened in that hospital room nearly a year ago, but he knew Nicholas had a big hand in Park's mental recovery, and because of that, he would forever love this brother in Christ. He included Nicholas in family dinners, even when Park was not there.

The Reward

Park's Jeep was in the shop, so she bummed a ride on the back of her partner's bike. They both stared in awe at the party of strangers gathered together at her house. Park waded through the throng in her living room to enter the kitchen.

Weasel turned around with his mouth stuffed full, "Suhpwize!" He swallowed and continued with a grin. "You never would have guessed would you? Have you seen it?"

"Seen what, Luke?" That was his Christian name.

"Your surprise. Come out here and see." He led her to the deck. "There she is."

Park feasted her eyes on a tremendous vessel with *Freedom's Park* painted on the side. Its double story cabin silhouetted invitingly to the new owner.

Grant Grayson approached her, "Well, Park, what do you think about it?"

"I don't understand," she gasped.

"The guys wanted you to know how they feel about what you did for them."

"But, I didn't do anything you and those other four soldiers did not do. You shouldn't have done it. It was all in the line of duty."

"Stuff and nonsense!" he grunted. "Now come, I want you to meet my son," he led her to a recuperating Shawn. His features were still filling out from the lack of food for so long, and his hair was just beginning to grow where it would. He was a fine soldier who had beaten the odds and survived where few men could. "This is my son, Shawn Grayson. Son, this is the woman responsible for all this."

Park reached her hand to shake his, "I am afraid, your father is being unfair, this was his project. It was he who planned and scraped to bring home his most precious."

"You are wrong Miss Park, my father has told me all. I know what part you played in this, and I know what part my father has played." His eyes filled with tears and his voice was weak. "I hope, someday, to repay you for what you have done."

"It is not by works, Mr. Grayson, lest any man should boast. It is not what I have done, but what God has done. He paid all debt for you and me."

"Well said," spoke the father, "and amen! Shall we go check her out?"

He took her hand and escorted her into the small motor boat that took them to the yacht.

Bruce and Christy picked up the girls from preschool for Park and brought them home. They went in one door and out the other to the lively party on the beach. The girls stayed in the kitchen with Nicholas, while Bruce mingled with these Army soldiers, reveling in his best friend's reputation.

"Is that boat for Momma's birthday?" asked Sarah.

"No, it is a gift for bravery," said Nicholas in surprise, "I did not know it was your Mom's birthday."

"It's not today, it's Fwiday, silly," laughed Anna.

Nick laughed and pulled her in his lap to tickle, "Friday, huh? Why did you not say so sooner, then?"

Sarah, trying to sound all grown up, said importantly, "Cause Momma don't like to talk about her birthday."

Nick stopped tickling, "Why not, everybody has to have a happy birthday?"

It was Sonya's turn to explain, "Aunt Park says that when babies are born, the angels all gather around heaven to see the miracle and rejoice."

"But sometimes," picked up Sarah, "When they see a baby born to sadness, and Mommies don't want them, the angels stand around crying for the unloved baby. Some people don't have happy birthdays, they and the angels stand around sad."

"I made her a pik-tour at school, wanna see it, Uncle Nick?" Anna interjected.

"I sure do Angel. Go get it."

"Sarah, would your Mom get mad if we surprised her?"

"I don't know, Uncle Bruce always just says, 'Let

her be, she'll be fine.'"

"My daddy has known her for years," Sonya accented the "years" by drawing it out, "and he knows everything about her. He told my Mom that the only babies the angels would cry over are the hearts Aunt Park will break."

Anna came back carrying a paper almost as tall as she and climbed back into Nicholas's lap. "What a pretty picture, Anna. Did you do this all by yourself?" he asked.

"Uh-hmm, see, theywes Mommy widing Spiwit, and me and Sawah and Tonya and Mafew."

Bruce and Christy reentered, "Man, have you seen that boat? It is nice. That was cool of them to do that for Park."

"It is nice." Nicholas handed the picture back to Anna to return to its hiding place.

At last, the guests were all gone, except Paul, who had arrived late. Park was exhausted. She cleaned any remnants of the gathering she could find and sank into the luxurious couch, where Paul pulled her feet into his skilled hands and massaged the tiredness from them.

She told him only a limited amount of detail about the rescue mission, otherwise he might get suspicious as to why his girlfriend was capable of such activity. He was proud as a peacock over his hopeful betrothed.

He had asked her to meet his parents next month, and she knew how serious this was. She had been contemplating this thought for a while and wondered if he could handle not knowing about her job. This might be something she would have to give up.

The question was, did she love this man enough to give up her job? Love? She had not thought of that before. She had never told him that she loved him. Did she love him? She certainly didn't feel the same giddiness she had felt with Matt, but no one could expect to meet two men in one lifetime that would love you the same, or you them.

Yes, she loved him. She loved the lines in his face when he smiled, and the way his hair tossed in the wind when they were on the ocean side. She loved to watch him around his patients. His bedside manner was kind and generous. Yes, she loved him, and tomorrow she would tell him.

He had murmured, "I love you", to her a couple of times, when he was not sure she was listening, since she made no reply. Tomorrow, she would!

Paul Douglas was ready to pop the question. Her eyes answered the question in his heart of whether she felt about him the same as he did her. She told him clearly that this was just another day, and he was to do nothing different. However, she agreed to a simple dinner.

He prepared for an elegant dinner fit for the fairest queen, because tonight was the night. He wore his finest navy blue suit, with a white rose peeping out of his lapel. He was a picture of total masculine beauty. Inside the lapel pocket, lay a beautiful diamond engagement ring.

His eyes reflected approval when Park opened the

door. She wore a yellow and white satin gown that changed her appearance to a spring flower, while her neck fashioned the diamond heart necklace in exquisite unique beauty.

Dr. Douglas felt regal with this beauty on his arm. He doted over her smile, and thrilled when she agreed to the opera afterward. That is when he would make his move.

He dared to touch her hand and keep his hand on hers. The magic of the night seemed surreal. Everything was working out perfect. During intermission, Paul asked Park to stroll with him in order to find seclusion to ask the question.

"You look incredible tonight, Park." He smiled charmingly. "You will not be offended if I tell you that I love you, will you?"

Her eyes met his dancing brown ones, while the words lingered on the tip of her tongue. She could not seem to release them, when suddenly, his pager went off calling him to the hospital. Was it Divine intervention?

Secrets

Park wakened early, and could not go back to sleep, so she decided to take her morning run. Since Sarah and Anna had stayed at Bruce's for the night, she escaped to the ocean's edge. She ran the three miles to the barn that housed her thoroughbred, with the idea, that she would exercise Spirit as well.

She spent an hour and a half stroking the magnificent beast until his coat shined. Spirit turned his long soft nose nuzzling her side trying to get his teeth on the carrot she had in her pocket.

She made a startling discovery, when she went for the saddle. It was gone! In its place, a new one straddled the stand, with the strong scent of new leather teasing her nostrils. A paper attached to it by a blue ribbon read, *Something special for Spirit, enjoy the ride!* The handwriting looked vaguely familiar, but she couldn't place it.

"Well, Spirit, looks like someone likes you a lot.

Look at this beautiful new saddle. I hope you will like it as much as your old one." She smoothed the saddle blanket, placed the new leather across his back, and tightened the cinch.

They were off in the earliest rays of the sun. She rode down the coast to a place where she knew some pastures and woods invited hikers and riders. Spirit was proud to have his master on his back. It was one thing for the stable hands to exercise him, when Park was unable, but this was his master. She was gentle in handling, never used a whip, and never jerked the reigns.

Christy brought the girls home, while Park was out riding. Anna hastily brought her picture to the table for her mother, and Sarah placed her handmade card with it for their mother to find when she came. They had to leave before the mistress of the house returned to meet Bruce for lunch.

Park had utterly forgotten it was her birthday until she breezed in to the kitchen. A tearful smile covered her lips to find such precious tokens of love from her girls. She carried her treasures to her room and put them on her dresser.

In concluding her shower, she heard those dearest to her come running in, so she hastened her dressing.

"There are my little sly ones. I missed you so much. Give me a hug," laughed Park.

"We came earlier, but you were out," explained Christy.

"I went riding this morning. I am sorry. Did you girls behave?"

"Yes ma'am," puffed Anna, "I was special good Mommy, I sitted wif Mafew fowa Cwisty."

"And did a very good job, might I add," said Christy, "Did you have a good evening with Paul?"

"Very nice, until he was paged and had to leave in the middle of the opera."

"What's with your flowers?" Christy gave a curious look past Park.

Park spun around to find a trail of daisies calculatedly placed in a path from her kitchen to the deck table. The remaining daisies surrounded a silver covered dish. "I know nothing about this. I just came out of the shower."

"Well, see what it is then?" exclaimed an excited Christy.

"Okay," Under the silver lid posed a cake. Gumdrops embedded the icing spelling the words 'Cherished One'.

She puzzled for a brief moment. The fact that Christy was here at this point was a little too convenient. She smiled for now she had proof that Christy was her flower bearer. She couldn't let Christy know she knew her secret, so she decided to play along.

Maiden Voyage

Freedom's Park was a drifting cloud. The high seas tossed all around them. The great sea captain, Bruce Clayton, was at the helm. His specialty may be planes, but he was no amateur with boats.

Park wanted to take her gift on a trial run, so she engaged Paul to run out with them for the day. His caseload was light, and he could play hooky.

The girls could not contain their excitement, because they were going to fish for dinner and swim for fun. They thought Paul looked funny, when he showed up at the marina donning his yachting attire with fishing pole in hand.

After cleaning up the dinner dishes, they all hopped into the water. Park taught the girls some basics about diving, while Christy held Matt on an inner tube on top. Everyone else took turns going down to the bottom.

The girls did not venture far. Paul and Park went

down alone to find some shells to bring back to the children. Finally, Bruce and Christy tried it next, while Park watched her husband's namesake.

They all sat back in lounge chairs to watch the sunset from the midst of the vast ocean. They had experienced a much-needed day of relaxation and fun. Now, the moon left a trail of silvery white upon the calm waters.

Paul searched for the perfect time to ask Park the question that had been burning in his heart for so long, but found no such occasion.

***

It was late when Park arose the next morning, and she had to rush to get to church on time. She was unable to attend her favorite church up in the mountains, so she resolved to go to the one Bruce attended, a little way down the road.

Richardson interrupted the service with a phone call, and she had to leave mid-service. Bruce and Christy assumed custody of the girls when Park slipped out.

Her commander sent Nicholas and her overseas to find a nuclear gas that the terrorists were threatening to release. They were successful in ferreting out the people that were responsible in just under a week; they secured the gas and had the perpetrators in custody.

Back at headquarters, Park showered and changed into clean clothes that she kept there. It was four o'clock in the morning and too early to get the girls, so she invited Nicholas to have some coffee with her. Not wanting to go home quite yet either, he agreed.

They found an all night diner that served a drinkable cup of coffee. The water, however, was not for human consumption, and for the first time since Nicholas had known her, Park drank coffee. She snarled her nose up as she drank the bitter cup.

"I really don't see why people drink this stuff," she joked. "It does not even taste good. If something tastes so bad you have to make yourself drink it, there is something wrong."

Nicholas laughed, "I guess you are right. It is an

acquired taste."

Park stretched her legs across the booth seat and leaned her head against the wall. "Sometimes, in the early hours of the morning, I imagine I hear the shower running, and I think for a split second that Matt is getting ready for work." She closed her eyes. "I declare I can still feel his presence at times. For example, when I am laying in bed at night I can feel his breath on my face."

He spoke in admiration, "You really loved him. I have seen how you grieved over the loss of your husband."

"It is not as bad anymore. I mean, after this long, you grow adjusted to being alone. There are just moments that are harder than others."

"You two were married for what, three or four years?" He took her cue and turned in his seat, playing with his coffee mug.

"Three and a half. He is the only love I ever knew."

"How did you know," inquired her friend, "I

mean… that he was the man you wanted to spend the rest of your life with?"

"When I was sixteen, Matt came to the group home that I lived in. His mom died giving him life, and his dad just left him at the hospital and disappeared. State put him in a home for a few years, but the dad in that home used him for a punching bag." Nicholas watched her stroll through these memories with an expression of adoration on her face.

The waitress interrupted to offer more coffee.

Park continued softly and tenderly. "On holidays, he and I were the only ones with no home to go, so we hung out together at the home. I thought he was the cat's meow from the first. He was a year older than I was, but he had failed a grade, so we were together in that aspect. I was a scrawny little kid that he wouldn't look at twice, but I didn't care. I idolized him. He was my hero. I received a lot of torment from the kids at school, but he would somehow appear out of nowhere and scatter

everyone. They left me alone when he was around."
She curled her nose up, as she place the coffee mug
to her lips. "Our senior year, he found Christ and
changed. He grew up a lot. He forgave his birth dad
and lost so much hate."

Nicholas smiled. "There is nothing like finding
salvation to change your whole attitude. Is that when
he fell in love with you?"

"I don't think Matt ever *fell* in love with me. He
was too distinguished for some crush. We began
dating in college. Bruce, he and I determined that we
were going to make the world sit up and take notice.
We had a point to prove, so we joined the Air Force.
Since Matt and I had no family, and Bruce's parents
couldn't afford to send him to college, it was the
most logical solution."

"Seems to me, you had your heads on straight,"
Nicholas interjected.

"Matt did. He was brilliant. He earned his
Bachelor's a year ahead of everyone else, which
enabled him to advance immediately to Major, and

within a minimal time, was promoted to Colonel. He was awesome. He challenged me to work harder in order to keep up with him."

It was seconds before Nicholas spoke in a somber tone, "Have you always been able to get what you want?"

"What do you mean?" she puzzled.

"No one is able to refuse you anything, myself included."

Park was not sure how to take his comment. She couldn't respond. Is this what her partner thought of her, a spoiled brat that had to have everything her own way? Nicholas could no longer contain his mischievous grin and burst forth with boyish laughter.

Park retorted comically, "You are so mean, Nicholas O'Ryan, and I am never speaking to you again."

"Listen, if I looked like you, I would get everything I wanted, too. You wanted Matt, you got Matt. You wanted an education, and you got an education. You wanted a better life, you got a better life. All I am saying is you seem to get what you want in life. Me, I can't even get a decent cup of coffee."

Park didn't take the compliment offered, "You think having a pretty face is all glamorous? Well, it is not. People use you for the trophy you appear to be. The entire world can think my face is pretty, but the only ones that ever counted, saw me as hideous. I was so pathetic that my own parents found me unlovable, so looks don't really matter."

"Is that why you lived in foster homes?" his voice became gentle.

There was a far away expression on his partner's countenance. "I used to think that I would give anything if I could just have my Mother look at me and tell me that she loved me." She paused for an instant, snapping back to reality, "Then I grew up, and here we are."

The Proposal

Dr. Douglas had worked all night and was driving home, when he saw his future fiancé with her partner having a seemingly cozy confidence. He did not know why this bothered him so much, but he must find a way to work through this awful feeling. He went home to a restless sleep, deciding he needed to make the time to propose to Park, no matter what. He had to work again tonight, but he had the next three days off, and he would do it then.

The following morning, Park answered the doorbell four times to a florist bringing Paul's white roses. The afternoon rings went unanswered, because Park was gone. Richardson called her in on another assignment, much to Paul's chagrin.

He lost another chance to ask her, again. He sat down to write her his proposal in a letter, but ripped it up ten minutes later. Next week she would be going with him to meet his family. He could just as well wait, as not.

She returned from her mission two days later and surprised him at work. He grinned upon seeing her.

"Do you have to work tonight?" he asked over the cafeteria table.

"Not as far as I know, but one never can tell. Will you come for supper?"

"It will be late when I get off," he lowered his head.

Park smiled her charm, "How late is late?"

"Around nine."

"Come on by, I will keep a plate hot." She returned.

Park had a time getting the girls to go to sleep. They wanted to see Paul first. They were dreaming sweet dreams by the time he drove up at nine thirty. True to her word, Park kept Paul a hot plate ready for consumption, the minute he arrived.

"Walk out to the water?" he asked stuffing, the last bite of pie in his mouth.

"Sure. It is getting cool. You might need your jacket."

He wrapped his arm around her and led her to the shoreline. He had rehearsed all day for this moment, and now it was here. "Park, you know that I love you. You know that it is real. I have come to consider you a lot more than a girlfriend. I want to ask you...will you..." he fluttered before spitting out, "Park, I love you and want to make you happy for the rest of your life. Will you marry me?"

Park was ready to respond, because she had anticipated this moment. She opened her lips to say, 'Yes', but when the words came out, she said, "Paul, I am honored that you have asked. Will you give me some time to think about it?" She was as shocked as he was at the involuntary words, but then she added, "That doesn't mean the answer is no, so don't look that way. I have been married before, and I lost my husband. I have to be sure I am ready to start over again in such a big commitment. Please try and understand."

"If it doesn't mean no, then will you at least keep the ring until you decide? When I see it on your finger, I will know your choice." He presented her with the tiny box. The ring was exquisite.

The Confession

Park was not sure what had stopped her from accepting his proposal, but in a way she was glad she did. She needed a sounding board to figure this out, and since old faithful had Christy, she didn't talk to him much about things like this anymore.

She chose to go riding. That always cleared her mind. Spirit could listen to her rambling, and God could answer her fears.

The next morning, she called her partner, inviting him to an outing. The two met at the stables after Park deposited the girls at preschool. Nicholas stood by his motorcycle with his arms crossed, as Park walked toward the stables.

She realized he wasn't following her, "What is wrong, Partner, aren't you coming?"

"I am not going in there with those animals," he growled.

"Don't you like horses?"

"Nope!"

She laughed melodiously, "Are you saying you have never ridden before?"

"Nope!"

"Well, now is a good time to learn. It is no different than riding that bike." She pulled his folded arms.

"Nope!"

"Come on you big chicken. I will give you Sarah's pony. He will be gentle."

He hesitantly yielded to her pulling him to the barn, where she showed him how to groom the animal in order to become acquainted with it and taught him how to put the bridle and saddle on. He almost fled when it came time to mount, and if it had not been that the woman he admired would think less of him, he would be long gone.

The horses walked, and then trotted together down the beach, to the field on the edge of the woods where Park liked to come to be alone. She posted elegantly, while Nick flopped around holding on tightly for his very life. After dismounting, Nicholas walked dramatically to show his discomfort.

"See, you survived," said Park pulling him to the ground.

"I will stick to the motored kind of animal, thank you very much. Next time, forewarn me that you want me to commit suicide." He fell back as if he were dead.

Park gathered some purple clover flowers, and showered them upon his face, laughing. "Oh don't be so dramatic."

He quickly grabbed at her arm, but missed it. Then sobering, he asked, "What's up friend?"

"Does something have to be up for me to enjoy a day with my friend?"

"I know that look on your face. Something is bothering you. Do you want to tell me?"

She lay on her back putting her head next to his head. Her blue dress brought out the prettiness of the blue in her eyes. Thinking aloud, she spoke, "How come you never got married, Nicholas?"

"I guess the right one just hasn't come along yet. I could not marry someone unless I really loved her, and she loved me."

"And you never found anyone you wanted to share your life with?"

"I did once, but it did not work out. She did not feel the same about me as I did her."

"I'm sorry, but I agree with you about what you said about the love part." She was quiet for a minute, "Paul asked me to marry him last night."

Nicholas fell silent as his heart dropped. "Congratulations," was barely audible.

"No congratulations, yet. I didn't say yes."

His heart rate increased, "How come? I thought you were pretty crazy over this doctor."

"I thought so too, until he verbalized the question, and then..." she trailed off. "I have these feelings for another man that I shouldn't have. If I love Paul enough to marry him, I should not be having these feelings for anyone else. I love Paul, I just do not know if I am *in* love with him. Maybe it is just that since I lost one husband, I am gun-shy to have another. Am I imagining trouble when there is none?"

His heart fell. There was, yet, another man. She would never love *him*. "Have you taken it to God? He will give you the answer." His tone was cold.

Before Park could reply, the phone rang, releasing the bonding. "Yes. Alright." She hung it up, "We have an assignment. Time to go."

Truths Be Told

This operation required them to go to Chicago, to intercept military weaponry, being smuggled by way of the black market. The informant, Doherty, risked his life by turning traitor and insisted on full protection every minute. Park played the part of Doherty's girlfriend, Candy, and Nicholas would remain behind the scenes, unless need be.

Park smacked her gum as Doherty introduced his "chick" to the little snake-like man. He fairly hissed when he spoke, reminding Park of that forked tongued creature. She twirled her hair and acted bored and disinterested, while they disclosed location and came to terms on payment.

She was startled to hear, "Park?" and looked up into the questioning eyes of Paul.

"You got the wrong person, Mister" she smacked her gum through her words.

"Abort! She's been compromised," Zoe

267

commanded on the communications device. "Get them out, Nick."

Paul, who had come to Chicago for a convention, was troubled to see her here. Who was that sleazy looking man who kept his arm around her in an intimate manner? After his fellow doctor left, he stormed over to find out if this was the reason Park had refused his proposal. He continued angrily, "Am I to believe that this is what you'd rather have than me? This..."

Park reached up and placed a fist between his eyes that put him to the floor. She had to shut him up for his own safety, and that was the only way. She turned around to face a cold steel.

"What is all this Doherty?" hissed the little man.

Park didn't hesitate grabbing his arm, twisting it until he dropped the gun and placed a perfectly executed kick to the man's head, rendering him unconscious.

Nicholas approached and pulled Doherty away. He threw the snake man over his shoulder, and when

Paul regained consciousness, he looked around in confusion, because no one was there.

Back at headquarters, Richardson paced back and forth. The door barely opened before he ordered, "Stevens, my office, NOW!"

She silently followed the irate boss.

"Do you have any idea what we do here? Do you know how many lives depend on us? You have jeopardized Doherty, Nicholas, and every person in that restaurant today. If this mission had failed, civil war would break out in the countries that are buying the guns. You are not some school-age teenager with a hormone problem. If you cannot keep your personal life separate from your work, then you don't need to work here. I cannot believe an agent with your background could be so stupid as to link up with someone on the outside who doesn't understand a thing we do here. Now, get out of here! I will decide if you are worth risking another incident or would we just be better off cutting you loose."

"Yes sir," she fought back the angry tears that

threatened her. She had disappointed Richardson. She could handle him yelling at her, but she could not deal with him being disappointed in her.

She left in a state of bewilderment. She didn't even hear Fred calling to her as she left. Zoe had told him what happened, and he wanted to tell her it would be all right, but she marched on.

Park passed her Jeep and kept walking, until she found herself on the beach going toward home. There was something about the ocean that made the omnipotence of God seem so real. Fear crept into her heart. How had this happened? She had prayed for guidance and wisdom, and received none. She yearned to jump into the waves fully clothed and just scream it out of her system.

Meanwhile, Nicholas filled out his report and went straight to Park's house, because he knew she would need a friend now. He heard Richardson yelling at her through the closed door.

Paul came straight from Chicago to Park's house. Finding she was not home, he wandered to the beach to wait, where he found Nicholas waiting on her deck. The two men glared at one another in a primitive anger.

Paul was the first to speak, "Does someone mind telling me what is going on? Park says she is not Park, then she decks me, then she disappears, and now you are here. That shouldn't surprise me, though, you are always hanging around."

"You just wouldn't listen to her would you? You almost got her killed back there," a furious Nick responded.

"I didn't know. I still don't know. Why was she with that slime ball?"

"That is her job. That is what she does."

"She's a prostitute?" he emitted.

Nicholas could feel his hands turning into fists. "She is a government agent. She was, anyway. She will probably lose her job over this. She was undercover, and you blew her out of the water. You might as well have pulled the gun on her yourself."

Paul held his hurting nose. "Why didn't she just

tell me?"

"Because, when you are a secret agent, it is supposed to be a secret; hence the 'secret' part. I cannot believe you."

"Will she really get in trouble?"

"She was in the boss's office when I left. You could hear him through a closed door if that tells you anything." Nicholas descended from the porch and approached his bike, "Tell her I will come by later."

Paul was still standing there when Park came up the beach, a while later. When she approached, he felt worse. She wasn't angry with him. Instead, she was apologizing for hitting him, which made his guilt overtake him. He loved her too much to put her through this.

"Park, I found out something about myself today that I don't like. I have this problem with jealousy when it comes to you. I can't seem to control it, and it turns me into the monster you saw today."

"You were not a monster," she argued.

He continued without giving her any leeway.

"Yes, I am. It rages inside of me. I saw you with that cretin, and I wanted to hurt him. I was even more jealous when I came by tonight, and your friend, Nick was here."

"Nicholas was here?"

"I have seen the two of you together. I want you to look at me the way you look at him, but I realized just now, that you never would. You would not tell me you loved me, and now I know why. You love him."

"You are wrong, Paul. Nicholas is just a very good friend and my partner."

He insisted, "It is far better to end this now, before your feelings for me turn to hate. I am sorry, please forgive me." He kissed her forehead softly, and before she could answer, his long strides had taken him away.

Mysteries Solved

Nicholas O'Ryan went home to be alone with God, on behalf of his partner, one more time. He prayed earnestly for the one he loved, until he felt an unseen Hand upon his shoulder and listened to the inaudible Voice, "It is time. Go to her."

Making one stop on his short journey to her house, he arrived on the beach side once again. She was sitting where Paul had left her, confused and ashamed.

He bounded up the steps in two strides, picked her up, and placed her on his bike. He pulled her hands around his waist before biking the miles up the beach to a hidden cave around an inlet. He drew her off the steel beast and into the opening of his hideaway.

Park startled at his boldness, but followed his silent directions anyway. The wind blew past with a cleansing power. It seemed to erase all the problems of the moment.

"How did you find this place?" she asked interestedly, while looking all around.

"I was just out riding my bike one day and fluked upon it. It is a perfect place to escape the hassles of the day. Here, let me help you." He cautiously directed her to a stone seat and dusted the sand from it.

Her windblown hair had fallen in places, and the blue dress cascaded fully around her, accentuating her curious eyes as she watched him. She was the prettiest mess he had ever seen.

He claimed the falling pins from her hair and softly placed the strands across her shoulders, while searching her face for the truth in her heart. He yearned to hold her close and tell of his great love for her.

Grasping for a topic, he tried to cheer her, "Richardson will not fire you. You have to know that. You are the best he has."

A weak smile crossed her lips. "I don't mind so much losing my job, but I hate how I let everybody down. I put everyone in jeopardy back there. It was very stupid."

"You know, God has His reasons," he tried again. "Was Paul mad?"

"That is the worst part. Paul took all responsibility. It is my fault. I cannot be absolved from my actions that easily."

"Absolution is given by God. Paul probably realized what danger he put you in and felt badly. You and Paul can make it through this."

"I don't care about Paul and me. After a great deal of prayer, I know he is better off without me. My relationship with my Heavenly Father is the most important thing in my life. As far as a job, Kincaid recently offered me a teaching position at the base."

"Do not take any job offers yet, Richardson is not stupid enough to let you go."

They watched the colors of the sky begin to change into night. Nicholas felt a silent Nudge, and jumped to his motorcycle and opened the compartment under the seat. He continued praying without ceasing.

When he returned, he held out a single yellow and white daisy for his partner. Enlightenment spread across her face, as her eyes danced merrily, "You? You are my flower bearer? I don't understand. How did you know?"

"You told me one time you loved daisies. You said, 'Roses may be a classic, but give me daisies any day'. You told me your grandfather loved them, and that made them your favorite."

"Nick, I told you that on one of the first assignments we ever had, you remembered that?"

He knelt before her, "I remember every word that your captivating lips have breathed to me."

Another thought came to her. "The house in Montana, it is yours?" She shifted to her knees to meet his tall frame in the sand. He said nothing, but she knew it was true. "You mean I treated you like a guest in your own home?"

"You treated me like a king," he whispered.

"The saddle and birthday cake was you? Why?"

He took her face in his strong hands, "Don't you know, Park?"

She nodded, "I need to hear you say it."

"I love you with all my heart. It has always been you. Whenever you enter a room, my heart leaps to my throat. You fulfill every dream. I have prayed for God to remove you from my heart, because I thought you loved another." He closed his eyes to feel the truth. "Is that what you wanted to hear?"

Her body trembled. She had not felt this way since Matt told her he loved her. Nicholas embraced her in order to stop the shaking.

He revealed to her that he had taken his vacation in Montana, a camping trip about the time Park was due to give birth. He had called Elizabeth to be midwife. The two sat enchanted in their love for one another, until Nick's phone broke the spell. It was work. He had to leave again.

Remembering the Voice she heard in the hospital, "I have given you two strong arms to rest in," she realized it was Nicholas!

Road Trip

Park was not ready to shout from the rooftops about her newfound love. She knew Richardson had been lenient on her so far, and if this had happened to anyone else, that person would be gone. As much as her mouth denied it, she loved her job, and didn't want to lose it. Teaching pilots would be monotonous, and she would detest that. She was exploding with this new development between her and her partner, but the analysis was that it would be best to keep it mum.

She was too excited to sleep that night, for her heart and mind raced with thoughts of the years of anonymous sweet nothings that Nicholas had done for her. In her unrest, she set out on a cleaning spree cleaning the house vehemently from top to bottom. She finished shortly before the rays of sun came in full blaze the next morning.

She delighted in Nicholas's phone call in which he

reaffirmed his glorious love for her and renewed that love all over again. He was going to be gone on assignment indefinitely.

He suggested that she and the girls go to Montana for a few days, until Richardson made up his mind about what he was going to do about her infraction. It took a little persuading for her to finally consent.

Park hesitated, but finally packed their bags and prepared for the journey west. She packed up *Dixie's Pride* with their suitcases and walked over to Bruce's office to let him know of her escape. He offered to take her to lunch, but she declined, briefly telling him about the episode of the aborted assignment and the parting of her and Paul.

"I am sorry about that. He's decent. You were not too hard on him, were you?"

"I am afraid I was," she explained, "I shouldn't let him blame himself for it all."

"He'll get over you. How many hearts have you broken, leaving them pining for just a look from you? He can get in line with the rest," teased Bruce.

"I don't think so. Just whose heart have I broken?"

"Danny Lester, for one."

"You mean that red headed guy from seventh grade? I don't think so," she protested.

"You knew he had the biggest crush on you," laughed her friend.

"He put thumbtacks in my seat!" she cried.

"He was flirting! Remember Ronnie Johnson, or Stephen Rhodes? What about Stuart Bishop? You wouldn't even look at them, because you had eyes only for Matt. Hence, your heartbroken entourage."

Park punched his arm, "You have been reading too many romance novels. Those boys hated me and were cruel to me. What about you and Diana Sorenson? Talk about a crush! She would make you cupcakes and cookies all the time."

He retaliated, "Yeah, and she gave me three cavities with all her sweets. My dentist thanked her. Boy, that was a long time ago."

"Too long, and now, there is no Matt to stop them

from putting thumb tacks in my seat or stranding me on top of the tower."

"You still miss him?"

She sighed off the subject to begin another, "We are going to take a trip to Montana while Richardson decides whether he is going to give me the ax or not."

He looked surprised, "You are? How long are you going to be gone?"

"Probably just a week or so. We are flying up this afternoon."

"Now, don't forget school starts in two weeks."

"I don't think Sarah would let me forget kindergarten. Can you believe it Bruce, our little ones going to school?"

"We are getting old," he groaned. "Seriously though, do you need anything? Are you taking a phone this time?"

"I doubt it, but I will call if I get the chance."

He gave her a kiss on the part of her hair, "Be careful! See you when you get back."

Nightmares

She procured the girls from preschool before taking off. They stopped overnight in Missouri to break up the long trip, even though the girls were excited to get to their destination.

It was a dismal morning on Friday, but it did not slow down the process of flying much. By the time they reached Montana, it had stopped raining. Sarah and Anna ran and played in the yard. While mom prepared the house, they ran looking at the ducks on the pond and the rowboat on its topside. A rabbit chase ensued before they even entered the cottage.

They walked to the store for groceries, but Kevin drove them back, making Sarah and Anna befriend him for life. Now, they were set for a whole week.

The week of paradisiacal bliss consisted of fishing, boating, swimming, hiking, and hunting rabbits. Anna didn't like killing them, because they were her friends. Mom taught Sarah how to aim at the target.

Teaching them responsibility for weapons was an important parental job that Park took serious. She never left a gun where either of her girls could reach it. She always locked the guns in a cabinet with the bullets somewhere else. Both girls knew that guns were for emergencies and adults.

Monday brought more daisies to her door from Nicholas. She had time to miss him, and this brought him closer. She smiled as she played with their petals. Her heart was skipping. He had done all this for her, because he loved her.

She was not sure exactly when she had fallen in love with him, but she knew, now, that was the reason she did not have liberty to accept Paul's proposal. Paul! She would have to send his ring back to him when she returned home. It was very expensive, and she didn't want to be responsible for it.

Thursday's hike brought a surprise for the three, when they came traipsing out of the woods. Walking across the yard, in long swift strides, strolled Nicholas. He was ruggedly handsome in his blue jeans and flannel shirt. He wore a grin to greet his lover.

Still cautious of anyone seeing, he regrettably restrained from any outward showing of affection. However, Anna jumped into his arms, and he lovingly captured her and smothered her in kisses.

Always the gentleman, he insisted on sleeping on the couch, regardless of Park's suggestion that she bunk with the girls and give him his own bed.

At four o'clock Nicholas was still awake, thinking of the plans he had made for the three girls sleeping in those two rooms. His heart would not let him rest from the joyous tumult of being so close to her. God had heard and answered his prayer and given him the only woman he had ever thought of caring for. He wanted the responsibility of protecting these three, whom he loved so much.

Sarah entered his vision and paused his thought. "Do you need something, Sarah?" he whispered when he realized she was actually there.

"No, but Momma will," she yawned, sleepily stumbling toward him.

She was so grown up for a five-year-old, "Is it something I can do for her?" Nick asked indulgently.

"Momma has these dreams. They started after her accident. She don't remember them, but they're bad."

"What makes you think they are bad?"

"She cries and talks and hits."

"What does she say?" He patted the couch beside him for her to sit down.

"Sometimes she talks about her Daddy."

"And she don't remember the dreams when she wakes up?" He was trying to piece all the information together.

Their conversation ended because of the stirring coming from the other room. Sarah left Nicholas's side and went to her mother.

"Momma," she shook the sleeping mother, "Momma."

Her mother turned over, "What is it, sweetie?" she asked sleepily.

"Can I get something to drink?"

"Sure, let Momma get it for you," she started to get up.

"That's okay, Momma. I can get it, you just go back to sleep. I love you."

"I love you, Sarah."

Fishing for Love

Sarah tiptoed to the kitchen and drank a glass of water to make the excuse true.

Nicholas motioned for her to sit beside him on the couch, where they sat in silence until they were sure Park had gone back to sleep, then Nicholas asked her if she wanted to go fishing. She joyously agreed, and the two slipped on their garb and silently went to the lake.

"Do you wake your Momma up like that every night?"

"When she's home, I do. The first time it scared me. I woke her up, and she got upset, so I never told her again what she said. I just tell her I need something to drink or I got to go to the bathroom, and she goes back to sleep and don't dream anymore."

"That is an awfully big girl. I am very proud of you. You take good care of your Mom."

"You do too," she snuggled under his free arm,

"Momma said you were the one giving her all those daisy flowers. She'd get so happy when they came. She said this was your place, too, and I think it was nice of you to let us stay here. This is where Anna was born, you know?"

"I do know." He tried to get back on the subject of the dreams. We ought to come up with a way to help your mom with her dreams, without you having to wake up every morning. When school starts, you will not be able to keep that up very long."

"Are you worried about Momma, too?"

"Now don't tell me that your pretty head worries about your Momma?" He hugged her to him, "You are too young to have that responsibility on your shoulders. How about if I do all the worrying about her, so you don't have to?"

"You ought to marry my Momma," she said in a grown up way. "With you she would feel safe even in her dreams."

"You know Sarah that is not a bad idea. Maybe you are on to something here. You reckon your mom would want to marry me? It could be a problem, if she did not want to marry me."

"If she don't, I'll marry you, and you can take care of her," proposed the little girl.

Nicholas laughed, "That sounds like a superb plan! Shall I ask her?"

"I think she will," giggled the tired child.

"What about Anna? Would she like that?"

"Sure! Anna will do what I tell her to."

"Now Sarah, don't pick on your sister just because she is younger than you."

"Yes sir," she pouted.

"We need to have a plan to...Oh Sarah! Reel it in, you caught one! Here turn this. Oh my, that is a beauty. Here, let us put it on the string."

"I caught one!" she shouted in glee.

The two fished until daybreak plotting their little scheme. Sarah carried the three fish she caught with eagerness to show her mom.

Nicholas and Sarah huddled and whispered all day to make plans for this big shindig. Their plan called for Nicholas to prepare the fish they caught into a formal dinner, which Park agreed to attend.

Sarah insisted on putting daisies in her mother's hair. She brushed it until all the tangles were out, and pinned daises randomly throughout the mass of curly waves.

He had brought with him a white dress similar to the one he had seen her wear that night on Spirit. He told the sales clerk she was so big and held his hands to her size, and came away with a perfect fit. He bought her slippers the same way.

When she emerged from the bedroom, Nicholas's face froze in awe, without a smile. The lovely dress fashioned her to a wild queen daisy among the little kingdom of lesser ones in her hair. The cotton sundress fell ever so subtle across the top of her shoulder, revealing nothing but mystery. The yellow ribbon laced the front from waist up. Her white slippers had laces that climbed her leg reminding him of ivy. Her hair fell to its full length with a wild look of the mermaid creature that legend talks about.

"Is there something wrong?" she feared.

"Oh, Momma, you look so pwetty," said Anna. "Don't she look pwetty, sisturah?"

"Yep, come on Anna, let's get the drinks," responded the sister, retreating to the kitchen.

Nicholas was still speechless. She was a goddess who had turned him to stone because her beauty was so fatal. How could he ask her to marry him? Why would she want to marry an old lug like him? She was so elegant, and he was so backward.

"Nicholas, are you upset with me?" she poked into his thoughts.

"N-no," he stammered, "you look so...so..."

"Uncle Nick, fire!" yelled Anna.

"Oh! The supper!" he exclaimed as he ran to the kitchen.

Behold the fish that they had worked so hard to catch and clean burned to a crisp. His perfect evening was ruined.

The mother shooed the girls out. "Girls go outside. We can handle this." She tried to come to the kitchen to help, but they refused her entry.

He came back to her apologetically. "I am sorry. I burned supper. It was supposed to be perfect, and I ruined it."

She laughed, "No you did not. You only burnt one thing. Everything else is perfect, so we will eat that."

"But, I wanted it to be just right for you," he argued.

She stepped closer to him and responded with dancing eyes, "You are here, what could be more perfect? I am so glad you were able to be here...with us."

As they sat down to a wonderful meal, in spite of the burnt fish getting soaked outside the door in the torrential rain that had begun to fly from the heavens, Nicholas could not keep his eyes off his fair maiden. The time had come for his speech.

He nervously began, "Sarah, Anna, I know I am not your Dad, nor could I ever take his place. I am not trying to replace your Dad, but if your Mom

293

would have me, I would like to be a new dad for you. That is, I love your mother, and I would like to take care of her for the rest of her life, if that is okay with you."

"Yippee!" shouted Anna. "You can be my Daddy."

"How about it Momma, will you marry me?" His eyes did not leave hers.

Park thought her heart was going to jump out of her chest and reached her hand to stop it from doing so. A sudden look of horror replaced the angelic smile. The touch of her hand to her breast reminded her of her inability to be intimate with a husband. The scar that the devil put on her would make sure no man would ever want her again. It worked! How could she explain to this man that she was used, filthy, and ruined? He was too pure in heart to understand the implications of those wounds.

Nicholas's heart sank, as she pushed from the table and was out the door before one could blink. He looked from Sarah to Anna in dismay.

I Do... Not

Nicholas breezed through the door into the rain. He found Park behind the capsized boat by the lake and cautiously approached her, again drinking in her natural exotic beauty that even the rains could not wash away.

"I am sorry if I moved too fast," he began, as he sat next to her. "I never meant to scare you."

"It is not too fast. I just can't marry you."

"Why? I thought you felt about me the same as I do you. I will give everything I have to you." He realized that she had never said, 'I love you,' to him. "You don't love me, is that it?"

She could not look at him. "I do love you. My goodness, I never thought, after Matt, I could ever feel this kind of passion again. You just don't understand. There are things about me you don't know."

"You are right, I do not understand. If you love

me, what is stopping you?" He watched her flesh grow goose bumps from the cold rain that fell upon it.

She took so long to answer that he thought she was not going to. "Can you imagine what it is like to be so repulsed by the touch of your own flesh that you want to...to peel it from your bones and burn it? Or try to brush your teeth completely out of their gums, and rinsing with kerosene would not remove the vile? Or to vomit until you feel like every organ has removed itself from your wretched body? Do you know how it feels to scrub and scrub, yet the stench will not leave your nostrils, to feel the hands groping, and you are pleading with God to let you die?" Huge tears had welled in her eyes and begun falling down her already soaked cheek as she stared over the lake, but what she was seeing was far from the raindrops methodically pounding the hard surface of the lake.

He remembered finding her in the shower at the hospital. His heart began breaking for her torment.

"I know that I will be there for you in any capacity you need me to be," but she did not hear his promise.

"I couldn't figure out what I had done that was so horrible. I tried to be good. I tried never to make him angry, yet it did not stop him. Lisa would faint and become hysterical. I couldn't stand to see her in so much pain, so I...I would go in her stead. I suppose that makes me bad, because I chose to go."

He could find no words of comfort. He dared not touch her. He just listened. "When I found the opportunity to get out I did, but Lisa would not come with me. She was afraid. Now she hates me and blames me for it all. Truth be told, I may never know what else they did to her."

"You were both too young to have been at fault for any of it. You cannot blame yourself for things that happened then, and you are not responsible for Lisa. She had the same opportunity to get out as you did," he gently urged.

"Not really. I had help. God found a way for me to get out and He prepared a special place for me to store the memories without ever having to remember. I didn't remember it for years, until one day someone forced me to face it. I had to look at the reproach I had upon myself. For over twenty years there was not as much as a thought of it, until one day I forgot whom I was dealing with. I thought I could fight the devil and win. Without putting on the whole armor of God, I went to fight that battle, and the results of that loss is this is the reason I cannot marry you." Rising to her knees, she took her graceful hand and pulled the yellow strings of her wet dress to unveil the hideous scar as much as was decent.

Nicholas had seen the stitches and bandages in the hospital. He was not oblivious to what had happened, but he could not tell her he already knew. "I do not understand. I love you, not what your body bears. I hate that someone did this to *my* girl, but that does not change the way I feel."

"How could you ever want me? He did this to make sure no other man would ever want me. He gutted me like one of the farm animals we used to butcher."

Nicholas drew nearer, "Park, you can have all the scars you want, but you cannot change how beautiful you are on the inside. I did not fall in love with your body. Your beauty is deeper than an appearance. Your heart is huge and your love boundless. That is what I love. As for the horrible memories, we will make new happy ones, and soon all will be forgotten again."

"You might change your mind after it is too late," she protested.

He looked into her troubled eyes, "You might change how you feel about me when you get to know all about me, but I want to risk it. I love you that much." He sat her back down and leaned her on his shoulder. Neither one minded the rain that was beating fiercely upon them. "Park, may I ask you a question?"

"What?"

He gently quizzed, "Did your Dad do this to you?"

"It doesn't matter. It is over."

Nick's jaw tightened. Whether she admitted it or not, he knew the truth. How could this man roam free upon the earth after what he did to one of God's angels? "How come you do not have him put in jail?" he gritted.

"Because, jail is too good for him. God is the just Judge, and what He will recompense is far greater than anything I could do."

"But, I still want revenge."

"'*Dearly beloved, avenge not yourselves, but rather give place unto wrath: for it is written, Vengeance is mine; I will repay, saith the Lord.* Leave it to Him. It is all in His hands."

"And so is you being my wife. He is the One who put us here, in this place, right now, under these circumstances. You have to trust Him to lead us. He brought you to me when I prayed, and He knows my love for you is real. I want to take care of you come what may. You will be my wife, right?"

Again, there was silence for a span, with only the sound of raindrops hitting the wooden boat. This was all happening so fast. It was one thing when Paul proposed. For whatever reason, it did not reach the point that she needed to face this with him. Why did it bother her so much with Nicholas? She knew he loved her. She was putting him in a lose/lose situation.

It was not fair to reject him because of her inadequacies. He could love her in spite of herself. Slowly, she spoke into his ear, "If you are sure you still want me."

"You mean it? You cannot take it back now. You will marry me tomorrow, and make me the happiest man alive."

"Hold up a minute. We can't do anything like that now," she was excusing his veil of kisses.

"Why not?"

She put her hands on his face. "I am in hot water with Richardson. He is ready to fire me, and if I do one more thing to upset him, I am gone. He will never let me come back."

"I have the solution to that. We just will not tell

anybody."

"You want to marry me in spite of everything you learned today? You are wanting to marry me in secret, without anyone finding out, even Richardson? You do know that is impossible."

"Nothing is impossible with God. I am going to go tell the girls you said yes!" With that, he ran excitedly back to the house, dragging his reluctant betrothed behind.

The Wedding

True to his word, that night, when Park's dreams recurred, Nicholas was waiting to soothe her weary mind. When she began tossing and crying, he softly rubbed his fingers over her forehead. His touch comforted her subconscious horrors, as he kissed her lovely smelling hair.

Together, they sat in a chair beside her bed, with Sarah in his lap, and his hand on his beloved's wrist. With the comfort that she was going to sleep peacefully, and that she was going to be his wife the next day, he fell to sleep at last.

Nicholas had assumed Park would agree to marry him from the moment she confessed her love for him. It was no accident that he joined them on this trip. He had planned every detail down to the 'I do's'. He did not intend to leave Montana still a bachelor.

According to the arrangements with Kevin, a horse-drawn carriage pulled up to the front door that

Saturday morning. Kevin put some crude ornaments on the horse and carriage in an attempt to decorate it for a wedding.

Sarah and Anna's little eyes grew big, when they heard the sound of sleigh bells and peeked out the window. A quick finger to the lips, when they turned to Nicholas, squelched their desire to shout out in glee.

They were getting good at keeping quiet. He and Park sat them down and impressed upon them the importance of not telling anyone, including Sonya, about the marriage. They both promised whole-heartedly.

Per his order, Park was in the bedroom climbing into her, 'goddess dress', as he called it. Since the rain had soaked it, she was vigorously trying to press it, so she did not hear the bells.

Nicholas had bought Sarah and Anna new purple dresses for the occasion, but it did not take them as long to get ready as mom. She still had reservations about any of this. She stared unseeing into the mirror thinking. Was she moving too fast? Was this a mistake? No, God had given her a peace about this. She never would have agreed to it in the first place, if He had not settled it in her heart.

Having learned yesterday the secret to hooking the daisies together, Nicholas triumphantly gave Park a crown made of purple ones and white ones, when she came from the bedroom. The girls giggled at the crooked way he placed it on mom's head.

"That is okay, little ones. I made one for each of you," he laughed with them.

The groom wanted one thing in his love's life to be a fairy tale. The carriage ride displayed autumn beauty of the world's natural magnificence, but Nicholas could not remove his gaze from his mermaid queen.

The ceremony was a simple affair, with a short overweight preacher presiding over the ceremony in a little country church. Both improvised wedding vows, which proclaimed undying love for one another before God and man.

Mr. and Mrs. O'Ryan rode happily back to their little haven from the world and were preparing a celebratory hike when the call came for Nicholas to leave on assignment. Their first night together, would be apart.

The Request

Park received the fateful call a day after she arrived back in Charleston. Richardson ordered her in his office, and she hastily obeyed his command.

"I do not have to tell you how badly you messed up," he began, "or that if anything like this happens again, you will be fired on the spot. You are an asset to this division, and we cannot afford to lose you. You have one more, and I mean ONE more chance. I will be watching you like a hawk. Do I make myself clear?"

"Yes sir," she replied. She approached him ever so quietly, "Mr. Richardson?"

"Hmm?"

"Thank you," she sealed it with a kiss on his cheek.

"Go on!" he growled. After she left, he put his hand to his cheek and smiled. He couldn't let her go, no matter what brass said.

Nicholas returned and waited eagerly to begin their life together. Park picked up the girls, after finding out Nicholas had returned and brought his new family home to shower him with their love. It was an incredible new relationship for everyone.

Nicholas pinched himself the next morning to make sure his waking up in this heaven was real. There were two little bodies nestled between mom and new dad, soundly sleeping. He watched the smiles on their tiny faces, and then his eyes fell upon the peaceful face of his wife. She had not wakened at four in the morning last night. As far as he knew, she slept all night. He closed his eyes and began thanking God for His numerous blessings.

To throw off suspicion, he moved some of his clothes into his new home, but kept his old place. It was not long before the curious Bruce and Christy wondered why he was suddenly around so much.

They found it odd that he would be there before the dinners and remained until they had gone. He accompanied Park to their house every time. Bruce could see the look they would exchange, and he knew Park better than anyone did; therefore, he frequently asked her about how she felt about Nicholas.

She would always answer, "I am happy with the relationship I have with him now, why change it?"

They maintained the secret quite well, until one night an unexpected tapping on the back door sounded. Nicholas was taking no chances with his new wife and went to investigate. If some heathen from her past were coming to cause trouble, he would stop it before it started. He had his gun drawn when he came face to face with Richardson, who stared at him standing in his pajamas with a fleeting comprehension.

"O'Ryan, don't tell me...Here I thought all this time Park played the saint, and I find you in her bed."

Nicholas understood the insinuation of his words. He would rather they both get fired than for this man to misunderstand and taint his wife's testimony. "It is not what you think, sir."

"Oh, no? I doubt you are here in your pajamas, because you're sleeping on the couch."

"She is my wife, sir."

Richardson stood flabbergasted. "What are you talking about?"

"We were married a while ago," he explained.

"Why didn't you say something about it then?" In truth, Evan Richardson was hurt. He thought of this girl as his own, and she had kept this big secret from him. He would have given his blessing if they just had not deceived him.

"After the other incident, we felt it best just to wait until things cooled down, first," stated Park coming from upstairs. "We are going to have a public ceremony at a later time. We just didn't want to risk you being angry with us."

"May I ask what you are doing sneaking in our home at night, sir?" urged Nicholas.

"No! You may not. I came here to see Park, alone."

Park put her hand on her husband's shoulder, "It is

alright, Honey, I will be up in a few minutes. Mr. Richardson, it is a cool evening, let me get my robe, and we will take a walk. She returned post haste to her boss. In the safety of the dark, she continued, "Is something wrong, sir?"

"Park, what I say here has to be confidential. You can't even tell O'Ryan."

"Yes sir. Are you in some kind of trouble?"

"I think one of my superiors is in league with the enemy. I have had four failed attacks on the Freedom Rebellion situation. The only way this could be is if Intel is leaked prior to the assignments."

"What are my orders?"

"I am afraid it goes farther than that. I have tested positive for a gradual inducing drug. It is almost undetectable, but the doctor found traces in my blood. I should be fine, but if they find out I know, there may be another assassination attempt against me."

"What is it you want me to do?"

"Keep my back. I think something will happen

soon. There is a big commission happening in Brussels next week. If this is a success, my life will be in danger, and I intend to see that it is a success. You cannot do anything out of the ordinary. You are supposed to be on your toes from the Chicago episode, you can't change that. Continue as you have been, but be my eyes and ears. I will keep your secret, whether you do this for me or not. You are under no obligation."

She kissed his cheek, "It is taken care of. You have no worries."

"Park, you are the only one I can trust with this. Thank you."

On Special Assignment

Park flushed out the mole in camp with the use of her supposed alienation to help. It was a lot easier than she originally thought it would be. She reported to work one day to pretend that she was cleaning out her locker and turning in her weapons, when a coworker, Gaines, confided a brag to her that he would take care of old fossil fuel Richardson before too long and she could have her sweet revenge.

"He's been in charge for too long anyway. It's time someone retired the old man." Disdain seethed from his words.

She discreetly shadowed him to Brussels. There, Gaines followed Richardson unobtrusively. Outside the embassy, he lurked in the bushes, waiting for the signal to act. Further back Park watched Gaines.

Inside, Richardson watched his surroundings carefully. He scrutinized every action and reaction. The meeting seemed to be favorable for him, which meant the enemy would halt the proceedings, before finalization.

Several hours into the meeting, the mediator announced that it was time for the vote. A short, dark, thin man began passing around a syllabus for everyone to have one last look, before each made a decision. When he came to Richardson, he placed his hand on his back and whispered something in his ear. Within a minute, Richardson's face fell forward onto the syllabus.

Meanwhile, out in the dark shadows of night, Gaines waited patiently for the signal, and when the short, dark, thin man placed his hand on Richardson's back, he raised his sniper's rifle and took aim.

Before he could pull the trigger, though, Park put him out of commission with a quick maneuver. Quickly lifting her rifle, she placed a tranquilizing dart into Richardson's shoulder. She made one speedy call to the clean up crew, and as soon as she secured Gaines and ensured that Richardson was out of commission, she ran deftly to the window edge.

Inside, several of the men and women that were members of the committee had rushed to his side, trying to check for a pulse. One European man was slamming a gavel on the wooden podium. Park could not hear the words, but from the expression on the faces, she understood of the pandemonium inside that room.

She slipped carefully around the corner, but two men guarded the entrance. She must be very careful. Swiftly, she lifted a stone and threw it on the roof of the building across the way in order to make a distraction. One guard left his post to investigate, giving Park the opportunity to jump the other guard silently and enter the building.

Outside the door, she could hear the speaker almost clearly. "…to carry him out. We will reconvene in one hour to finalize this decision. Remember, ladies and gentlemen, we will not leave this place, until we come to a decision."

"Why so fast? We need to call the authorities," came another voice.

"I agree." This voice had a thick accent. "Vot is the rush?"

Then, the first voice sounded irritated. "I am tired of th..."

At that point, a noise down the hall caused Park to scamper. One of the closed doors down the way showed darkness underneath, which proved to be unlocked. This became her escape. She peeked out of the cracked door, until two men in medical uniforms pulled a gurney into the room.

Once more, she slipped out to the meeting room door. It was open, so she had to be careful. She heard hushed murmurings and was able to discern the, "Ready for transport," signaling her to take cover again.

She hid in the dark room, where she called a contact to intercept Richardson. She waited until the coast was clear to get close enough to see what was happening. She still had to determine who the bad guys were and how many.

She had barely finished speaking to the contact,

when she heard footsteps outside the door. They were coming toward her. Afraid to hide under the desk in the room, she deftly climbed into the windowsill behind a thick green curtain.

Three men and one woman entered, jabbering animatedly in a foreign language. Park dared not breathe for fear they would hear the faintest breath. Her brain raced to think of what she should do.

She was not fluent in their language and could only pick up pieces of their conversation. She did have the culprits she was trying to catch in this room, though. That, she knew.

She did not have to complete her thoughts, however, because several minutes later, an army of her colleagues burst through the door to capture the four criminals. Since she had not finished her phone conversation, she had not disconnected the call, and on the other end, Zoe heard the situation and dispatched the cavalry.

Everyone Knows

Christmas time came with an invitation to the annual benefit gala for the POWs. Park and her new husband reunited with a much happier Grant and much healthier Shawn Grayson. This year the committee decided to honor Matt for Park's sake and put up a memorial.

Nicholas reveled in his newfound family. He was excited to be spending their first Christmas as a family, but it went by all too quickly. He went a little extravagant with his gift for his new wife. He and Bruce went in together to buy a six-seated plane for the two families to share. Park and Bruce would have to further their pilot's training, but it would be a cinch.

For Nicholas, Park presented him with new birth certificates and adoption papers for both Sarah and Anna. She decided that Matt would want them to have Nicholas as their dad, if he could not be there.

They, too, wanted this very much.

Work continued through several more weeks
without anyone finding out about their secret
marriage, but it was bound to surface, eventually.

It happened one day while in the middle of an
assignment, when Park acted as a decoy for her
team's escape. The most important thing was to get
her squad to safety. At her command, the team left,
leaving her surrounded by gunfire. She took a bullet
in the leg, but continued fighting. No escape seemed
available.

Nicholas threw caution to the wind and raced in to
save his wife. Zoe ordered him to stop because it
was too dangerous for him to go in as well. Nicholas
ignored her orders. Again, she ordered, "Cease
advancement, now! O'Ryan, I have given you an
order. Cease, NOW!"

Amidst the bullets flying, Nicholas continued,
until he reached and covered Park. He defied a direct
order, but he did not care. Zoe could only hear

intervals on the communication system.

"Darling…hit…let me…" Nicholas instructed as he lifted his wife to his shoulder and sprinted through the gauntlet of bullets to safety.

Zoe looked at Fred, who wore a suspicious twinkle in his eye. "You know something about this?"

"I got eyes. I could see it coming."

Now that Richardson knew, it really didn't matter if everyone else found out. It had been fun trying to keep it a secret, but since the cat was out of the bag, they were free to tell Bruce and Christy.

At first, Bruce was hurt that they had not confided in him. He understood her need for secrecy, but could not help feeling a twinge of jealousy that another best friend had moved in on them. Besides, he knew something was going on between them already. At least, that is how he pacified himself.

In the end, he could not help but to congratulate Nick, with a friendly warning to take extra care of his friend. He liked Nick. He was a Godly man, and wise in the will of God.

He insisted that they have a second wedding up in the favorite mountain church, where he could give her away. Christy secretly hoped that Park considered her the matron of honor. Ulterior motives or not, Park would comply with the wishes.

They set the date, sat back, and let Christy plan the whole thing. "As long as you keep it simple," Park insisted. Christy enjoyed every moment of the planning stage.

She was becoming in her silver gown, with daisies in her long flowing hair and actual slippers on her feet. She did not wear combat boots to this wedding, but completed her outfit with the crutches the doctor gave her to use with her injured leg. Bruce helped her hobble down the aisle, to give her away.

All Nicholas could see was the woman who had vowed to be solely his until he died. This vision enthralled his soul. He knew he never deserved such a wonderful blessing as this, but he stopped to thank the Lord, right then. He completed the ceremony by reciting to his beloved, the words etched in his heart for only her.

Before leaving, the O'Ryans purchased a house, complete with guesthouse and pool, for a wedding gift to each other up in the mountains. Now, they had a place to stay on the weekends they chose to spend here, which meant they could come to church as much as they wanted.

They took their wedding trip on the ocean blue, aboard *Freedom's Park*, with Sarah and Anna in tow, but it had to be short, because Sarah had to return for school.

"Nicholas," they were watching the sunset in each other's arms, "you have told me about your mother, but you do not talk a lot about your dad."

"My father died when I was eleven. We were not that close."

"From what you have said, you were not that close with your mother, either?"

"No," he paused for several minutes, "I never could figure out why I felt I never belonged. She loved me and all, but there was something I just could not figure out, that made me so different. I just did not fit in."

"Was it because your dad died, do you think?"

"No, she revealed the reason on her deathbed, a few years ago."

"Why? What happened, then? Did you find out you were adopted?"

"No. Stolen."

Park's hand stopped midway up his arm in caressing, "What do you mean, stolen?"

"She told me that when I was a baby, my father kidnapped me so she could have a child. There was something wrong with her health, that she could not bear any children. She carried that secret all those years and said she could not die with that on her chest. She died before she could tell me any more." He was staring off into another world now.

"Did you ever try and find out who your real parents were?"

"For a while. I looked up all the three-year-old

boys that disappeared that year, and none were me."

"It is strange," mused his wife, "how some parents would do anything to have a child, and other parents would do anything to get rid of one."

He turned his lips to her ears, "I love you, darling. You are so wonderful to me. How would you feel about you and me having another one?"

She smiled until she realized he was serious, "Are you crazy?"

"I am serious." Park cupped her hands around his face, looking square into his eyes, to determine his heart. He *was* serious.

Originally

Nicholas's confession gave Park a new project to work at. The first opportunity she found to get away unnoticed, she began her search. It was five days of flying here and there and questions and misleads before she picked up the trail that she wanted.

She traced Betty and Frank O'Ryan's history to find where they lived when they would have acquired Nick. She picked up a couple of possible names, but neither panned out.

It was by the Unseen Hand of God that, when she started from scratch, and retraced the O'Ryans history a second time, she found a yearbook from his school.

She realized that the more she scrutinized, something did not fit. He looked so much smaller than the other children did.

He did not appear in any yearbooks before ninth grade. She asked a nearby student what she thought about the person in that picture. The girl confirmed that he looked like he was a couple of years younger than all the rest.

Giving Park an idea, she went back to the beginning to research again. This time, she found what she wanted and went back home with her findings to plan her next step. She explained to her husband that she was going to be gone a few more days on an assignment, and flew to Kansas.

With a briefcase in hand, she drove her rented car up the dirt road to a comfortable farmhouse placed on nearly fifty acres of farmland. She stepped out in her Air Force uniform with her bars and medals hanging in neat rows to a kindly gentleman sitting on the porch.

"Good afternoon, Mr. McCrain. How are you today, sir?"

He smiled a sad old smile, "Fine, ma'am."

"My name is Park O'Ryan," she extended her hand, "and if you do not mind, I would like to ask you some personal questions pertaining to your children."

"Ms. O'Ryan, what are you asking for?" asked the gentle man.

"In particular, about your son that was kidnapped thirty years ago."

A sadder smile took possession of his features, "Well, Ms. O'Ryan, there is not much to tell. He was kidnapped, and they never found him."

"I think I have found him, sir."

"Why should this matter to you?" he asked warily.

"Because, I believe your son is my husband."

"Daddy, what is going on here?" Park turned to see a hard young woman glaring at her. "We don't want what you are selling. My father's old, so please don't upset him."

Her father replied, "It is all right, Kathy. You can go on about your work," and she grudgingly left the two alone. "Please, I gave up years ago of ever finding my boy. He is dead."

"I have reason to believe he is alive. Here, look.

This is a picture of my husband when he was in high school. This is a picture of him, now. This one, I took a picture of your son from the newspaper and aged it over the computer. See the similarities. The hospital records show that your son had a birthmark on the back of his left ankle. My husband has the same birthmark. Your son had blue-green eyes, my husband has green eyes."

"It can't be. They said he was probably dead. How could you figure out what hundreds of police couldn't find?" There were tears in his old eyes.

"Well sir, I can only give God the glory."

Another saddened look crossed his face. "If he is my son, then why has he never come to us?"

"Because he never knew he was stolen until the woman that took him was on her deathbed. Only then did she confess to him. He searched for you himself, but they misled him about his age. He believes he is a year and a half older than he really is. That is why the authorities could not find him."

"Could it be true," he cried. "My wife grieved

herself to death after losing him. Oh Margaret, do you hear? He's been found. Tell me about him, please."

"Well sir, he is a fine, handsome, strong man. He is honest and good and Godly." The old man watched the enchanting woman's features as she described his son. She ended by saying, "If I may, there is one last thing that will verify it beyond doubt. May I take a sample of your blood? I have his on file, and I will have yours analyzed. This will confirm what we already know. He is your son." She smiled.

Park left the man in his fairy dream world with the promise to contact him with the results, and when she had the proof, she called him to prepare the reunion; however, she decided not to tell Nicholas yet.

She explained to the anxious old man, that the job she and her husband had required them to be out of town a lot, and it would be a while before she could bring him his long lost son.

It was three weeks from the original visit before

they were finally together for a few days. Park contacted Richardson about a few days off, and asked Bruce to keep the girls. Under the pretense of a vacation, Park flew her unsuspecting husband to that Kansas abode.

Once again, the old man was sitting on his porch. Knowing of their expected arrival, Mr. McCrain sent Kathy to town. Nicholas smiled curiously at the man as he ascended the steps behind his wife. What had she gotten him into now?

"Nicholas, here is someone you should meet," she turned to the man. "Nicholas, this is Albert McCrain. Mr. McCrain, this is your son, Nicholas O'Ryan.

A New Dad

Nicholas stared at his wife, then at the old man standing shakily with tears in his eyes. Astonishment stole any words from him, but Park simply smiled.

"It *is* my son. You have your mother's eyes," cried the man, reaching to embrace what he had lost. "Your mother had the same beautiful green eyes, and you have her color hair. Oh, Margaret," he looked toward heaven, "He's fine. He's home and safe."

Nicholas remained tongue-tied with an inability to speak. Park began to explain, "I have been researching from the information you gave me and, God led me to him."

"How could it be possible, I tried everything, and failed?" he asked weakly.

"Your origin was not the only thing Betty and Frank O'Ryan lied to you about. It seems that you are a year and a half younger than you always thought. She faked your birth certificate, but I am not sure how the schools didn't realize that you were younger."

He looked solemn and replied, "She kept me at home and taught me until I was in high school. Then, I just thought I was punier than the others were. I never dreamed any different."

"I found your picture in your ninth grade yearbook, and the Lord showed me from there. I met Mr. McCrain and obtained a blood sample. Fred ran it for me and it is a match," Park explained in excitement. Knowing these two needed time alone to reintroduce themselves, Park excused herself to put the plane to bed.

Nicholas still sat watching the old man who had begun asking innumerable questions. The years of worry began fading from his worn face. This was his son, who once was lost and now was found. It was time to bring in the fatted calf for a welcoming feast.

He told Nick how his mother had grieved herself to the grave when she lost her baby boy. The tones of endless love rang still in the old man's mention of

Margaret.

"Your sister, Kathy, and her husband live here with their boy and girl. Bob inherited this dairy, when his dad died. They aren't rich, but they hold their own pretty well. Kathy worries a lot about me. She sort of took the whole weight of this family on her shoulders and kept it together, well, what's left of it."

Nicholas contemplated each detail the old man offered, searching his mind for a memory of these people. Thoughtfully he asked, "Do I have a brother? I used to have this reoccurring dream that I was holding a boy's hand. I could not see the face or anything, just that I would start crying."

Albert McCrain's expression conformed to sorrow-stricken, once again. "My oldest child, your brother, was with you in the park one afternoon. He wanted to play ball with his friends. Margaret had told me not to let you go with him alone, but I made Tom watch you. He said he turned to catch a ball that was coming toward him, and by the time he turned back around, you were gone."

"I do have a brother," smiled Nicholas.

"Thomas felt responsible for your kidnapping, and in truth, I blamed him myself. He blamed himself for Margaret dying too. He thought we stopped loving him when you disappeared, and he could never love himself. He was twenty-two when he took his own life." The man was weeping for his second lost boy.

"I am sorry I caused so much trouble," stated Nicholas. "I wish I could have known my brother to let him know it was not his fault."

The conversation stopped for the time being, as Kathy came from the pickup that had just pulled in the drive. She came up behind Nicholas, "I saw that Air Force woman in town again. She hasn't been back out here pestering you again, has she Dad?"

She had not liked seeing the intimate huddle her father had shared with this strange woman. He would not tell her anything about the woman, which raised her suspicions.

"She has not been pestering me, Kathy. I wa..."

"I don't know what she is selling, but she better just go on back where she came from," she stated with finality.

Mr. McCrain became stern with his daughter, and he rarely did that. "You'll not speak that way of your sister-in-law, Kathy Barns, do you understand me?"

"Don't tell me she messed around with John and is now claiming he married her? What's her angle? You had better believe that if she was conspiring with John, she is up to no good. Daddy, I'm telling you, I will not have people taking advantage of you."

Stormy Weather

Nick faced the woman, but before he could say a word, his father spoke, "She isn't married to John, she's married to Nicky. Furthermore, she's not up to no good. You should be ashamed of your behavior. "His voice softened, "Nick, this is your sister who speaks before she thinks. Kathy, he has Mother's eyes."

She stared at Nicholas as if he were a snake. For the first time, she bothered to look at the man standing on the porch. He did have Mother's eyes, but his stature and other features reminded her of her father when he was a young man.

She still needed convincing, "I don't understand. Nicky's dead. People have given you false hopes for so many years. It is cruel to torment an old man." She directed a harsh stare at Nicholas.

"I am sorry if we have caused any inconvenience to your family," Nicholas said in cool politeness,

"My wife saw an opportunity to make me happy and heal old wounds. We would not want to impose on anybody or cause anyone any pain."

She ignored him, "Dad, we can't talk now. There is time for this later."

Dad looked at her puzzled, "Why can't we talk now?"

"Didn't you hear? There's a tornado spotted southwest and heading this way. We need to get ready. The kids are getting in the storm shelter. You get there, too. I have to help Bob. Hurry up."

Nicholas lost the argument of helping Bob and letting the woman stay safe, because he could not resist the pleading in the old man's eyes. Kathy ran to the pickup where she met up with Park.

She yelled to her, "Go get in the storm shelter. A tornado is coming our way!"

As Park drew near, she called, "So it is serious then? I heard someone say something, but I figured it was just a warning or something."

"No, it has touched down. I'm going to help Bob

get the animals."

"Kathy, you go back to those two men of yours, I will help Bob."

"I know what to do. There is a storm shelter out under the barn." Kathy insisted.

"Listen. We've no time to argue. There is a man in there that is not going to lose his sister the first day he meets her."

Kathy's face softened. "He is out in the grazing pasture."

Park sped the truck in the direction that Kathy motioned. Park grabbed some baling twine from the back of the pickup, tied each end to the sides of the fastest looking horse's halter, placed her hands on its rump, and in one graceful hop rode to Bob. The two worked swiftly to round the cattle and horses into 'Old widow Gravely's' silage pit for safety. It was a pit dug into the ground to store the winter's silage, but had been fenced in years ago, when they retired it from silage, to make shelter for the animals in storms. They raced back, on foot, to the pickup.

The wind was blowing hard now and the thunderous sounds were all around. The two were in the safety of the pickup at last, but they were not heading toward the house.

"Thanks for your help out there, I appreciate it, but I've got to run over to Old widow Gravely's and get her to shelter."

"Sounds like a plan, Bob," she replied without thought. "By the way, I am Park."

The road was blocked by a wind blown tree, making it impassable. Bob began looking for alternate routes.

"Is that her house up there?" asked Park.

"Yeah, I hope she's okay."

"I will run and get her to safety. You go back to your family. Is there any place I can get her to that is close by?"

"I can run, and you go back," he argued.

"Listen, Bob, you have a family to protect. We will be perfectly fine. No more arguments!" insisted the stubborn Irish woman. She had a command in her voice that one found hard to refuse.

"There's a cellar under her house made years ago," he explained. "It's been sealed from the inside because animals kept getting in. Outside in the back is another door. You should be safe there. Are you sure about this?"

Without leaving an answer, Park was already sprinting across the field to the woman's house. She entered without knocking and called out the widow's name. Searching all the rooms in both stories, she found no Mrs. Gravely.

She hustled outside to the barn, where she found her quest. The two clung to each other as they ran for the prophesied cellar, for the wind was strong enough to blow them away, now.

They hardly had the heavy wooden door barred before they heard the sounds of the tornado. Under the old colonial two-story house there grew a deafening silence. Finally, more tormenting sounds approached and then passed again.

The Aftermath

Bob had driven back to the storm shelter under the barn, where Kathy had come to terms with the news. He watched nervously as his wife and father-in-law reunited their lives with the son he had heard so much about. He watched the happy tears trickling down his lovely wife's face. She seemed so at peace for the first time. She opened up and shared about her life, her husband, and kids.

The kids watched every expression that crossed Nick's face in amazement. They, too, had been raised on the story of little Nicky who disappeared. This miracle enthralled them.

The kidnapper, Frank O'Ryan, took to his grave the fact that he had heard John calling for his little brother on that fateful day, as the boy frantically searched and called for hours. That is how he knew his name was Nick. Afraid that it might cause problems, they decided not to change his first name.

Not aware of this knowledge, the reunited gang considered it a miracle from God that he was still Nick.

The three old family members watched the new one as he described his life to them. It was a sad tale about a lonely childhood. He told of his Marine experience and finding complete happiness in marriage.

When he came to telling about his family, all sadness disappeared. His eyes filled with admiration, his heart with joy, and his voice with adoration at the mention of his wife. He told them she married him out of pity four months ago.

They did not even hear the tornado as it passed over, but the radio weather alarm intruded their talk. The announcer reported that the tornado dissipated seven miles north, northeast. All was clear.

They emerged from the hole in wonderment. The barn still stood, but was faceless. The outside opened to a huge yard, omitting the house they once had. Boards, beds, and all kinds of items lay in chaos across the path.

Nicholas and Bob went across the way to release two anxious prisoners from Mrs. Gravely's cellar. Fortunately, Mrs. Gravely's house stood in tact, except one side was gone. The tornado cleaned a clear path where it had traveled.

The collective families surveyed the ravaged land with a growing sickening in their bellies. Their house was completely gone and a few fences destroyed, which gave them occasion to spend the night in a hotel in town.

It was fun for the children, who rarely ever spent the night elsewhere. Bob and Mrs. Gravely squandered the evening away, trying to let the reunion complete itself. No one seemed to notice that Park was not there.

It was late when she retired to her room and climbed her exhausted body into bed after a hot shower. She closed her tired eyes to slumber and softly place a hand on her sleeping husband's arm. "Thank you, God, for Your blessings," she prayed silently.

"Park O'Ryan," she heard her husband's soft voice. "You are more precious to me than all the wealth of this world."

Park was a natural giver. She had the means to help others and did not hesitate to do so when the need arose. Her mind started racing the second she looked upon the damage of the Barns' house. She had in her power to help them out, so that her husband need not have to worry about the details. She wanted him to have no worries while coming to terms with all the changes in his life.

The following morning brought even more surprises. Each member of her new family awakened to all the necessary clothes and accessories down to toothbrushes. The children were excited at the fun they were having, but Mom and Dad were reluctant to accept these gifts from an anonymous giver.

Before breakfast was over, a contractor appeared and summoned Bob to a private meeting. He reported that he had been retained to rebuild the Barns' house ASAP. The instructions included that he was to get with Bob on any instructions.

The meeting concluded with Bob agreeing to pay him as soon as the insurance money came.

Park borrowed the pickup and disappeared again. She assisted their neighboring farmer in rebuilding his beaten fence. She was throwing the post hole diggers fervently into the ground again and again, when Bob sighted her from the rented car.

Bob smiled at Mr. Klimek with a, "How do you do?", but the German stood without speaking.

Nicholas, Bob, and Kathy approached Park in the field. "What in the world are you doing?" Bob asked.

"I am helping Mr. Klimek fix his fence. He lost some of his herd yesterday. If he doesn't get it fixed soon, he will lose more," she explained.

"He's never spoken a word to any of us. He is a cranky old rude buzzard, how did you get him to talk to you?" asked Kathy.

Nicholas reached his arm around Park's shoulders, "My wife can charm the bees from their honey?" he laughed.

"Hardly," Park's laugh rang sweet. "He doesn't speak English."

"You mean all this time, and that is why he doesn't talk to us? Well, don't I feel stupid!" exclaimed Bob.

"Come on, I will introduce you." She led the way and made the proper introductions in German and English, bonding neighbors for life. Mr. Klimek was a loner who needed only his wife to keep him company, and never desired to expand his English. Mrs. Klimek spoke enough English to get by for the both of them.

The others joined in on the fence mending. In exchange, for the repairs, Klimek agreed to watch the Barns' livestock, until they returned. Park financed the materials for the fence as partial payment of the task, and before she left, sent him another small amount for his service.

Going East

The final surprise was that the Barns family would inhabit the North Carolina mountain house until they could have theirs rebuilt. This took some persuading, but they finally gave in when Park made them realize they had nowhere else to go, and it would not cost her and Nicholas a thing.

It came about by an invitation for a vacation in the cool mountain air. No one, but Bob, knew the real reasons for Park's invitation. Kathy did not want to impose on this newfound brother and his wife, but Nicholas insisted.

"What is the point of having money, if you cannot spend it on necessities for those you love?" he asked.

The word "love" warmed the cockles of Kathy's heart, and then, she could not refuse her father the pleasure.

They loaded Park's plane, making Hazel and BJ double in one seat. This was the first trip east that anyone in this family had taken. It was a sight different from that of their native Kansas.

The new brother introduced them to the Blue Ridge Mountains from the air, giving the visitors first hand understanding of how they got that name. The blooms of spring were in full performance for the mid-landers.

She was genuinely happy for him, contrary to her own misery that was now only a matter of miles a way. Her family, for lack of better terms, was the proverbial thorn in her side that God, in His infinite wisdom, chose not to remove. Through it, she had learned of mercy and grace. She rarely visited her hometown without the flood of memories rehashing.

Nick watched his wife with a wave of appreciation consuming him. It seemed everything his goddess touched turned to gold. Even the flowers seemed to bloom just for her.

His world was completely full of joy abounding, yet he took time to wonder if his wife and work partner was as joyous as he was. According to her smile, she was, but he knew Park was not one to talk of such annoyances as unhappiness. She would accept her lumps and turn them to gold.

"Thank you, God, for this my blessing," he prayed silently.

As it happened, work called Park in for an assignment in the early hours of the next morning. She was en route to her destination when the satisfied new family awoke in the main house.

When the morning broke bright and fair, Nicholas rustled up the provisions Park procured for the morning feast before her departure. The aromas penetrated the upstairs floor, bringing a sleepy Kathy to help.

She put her arm around her brother lovingly, "Good morning, Nicky."

"Good morning," he smiled, "did you sleep well?"

"Like a dream. This house is marvelous. Park must be proud of it."

Nicholas turned the pan from the stove to empty the bacon on a plate, "You hungry?"

"You did all this? You should have called me, I would be glad to help."

"Park did most of the work before she left. I just had to throw it together." He could not hide the adoration in his voice.

"Left? Where in the world has she gone to this morning? Please don't tell me she went shopping for us again. She has already bought us enough clothes for the next five years."

Again, he smiled, "No, she had to go to work."

"Work, who's at work?" asked the father, coming down the stairs, rubbing his head.

"Park had to go this morning," Nick said reverently to the new father.

"Why in the world would she have to go in to work this early on a Saturday morning? Where does she work?" said the man to his son, while sitting at the table.

Nicholas knew he didn't have the liberty to disclose this information to anyone, which would be tricky, for he wanted to please his father. Greater

350

was the need for safety, though, than the need to be accepted, so he hedged carefully around it. "She is semi-retired from the United States Air Force. When the government calls you to your duty, you wait for no one," he passed it off jokingly.

Bob, Hazel, and BJ made their appearance at the feast and heard the explanation. Bob stood behind Kathy's chair, putting reassuring hands on her shoulders, and said, "Say, Nick, where did you find her? She is special, isn't she, Kathy?"

Nicholas simply responded, "I prayed to God and asked Him for her."

Church

Sunday morning was rainy, but the crew set out to the best church in the world. Nicholas had never been to church here, without the adornment of his bride before, so this was a new experience for him.

Not much did the Barns family or Albert McCrain worship, since they had grown angry with God for taking their little Nicky and then their beloved Mother and brother, but they proudly followed Nicholas to one of the front pews, glad to be in worship as a family, at last.

Most of the men, women, and some children gathered in the front of the church, after the choir came down from the singing, bowed on their knees, and began praying aloud in unison. The altar prayer lifted the voices of men and women to the highest courts of Heaven for the purpose of the Advocate to take to the Father. This was different from any experience the newcomers had ever seen.

One man sang a solo, after the ushers gathered the tithing. His strong voice rang out a beautiful melody about how the blood of the Lamb had enough power to cleanse even a wretch like him. It was enough to send cold chills all over Bob, who drew his arm closer around his wife.

When the preacher called the next special singer, Park and two little girls approached the piano from the back of the church. The little girls sang with a beautiful conviction.

Kathy reached over and whispered to Nicholas. "Who are those girls with Park?"

"Those are our girls," he replied proudly.

After they sang, Park and the girls took their positions by Nicholas, but Kathy looked in puzzlement from one to the other all through the service. She heard very little of what the preacher said. There was so much to absorb is such a short amount of time. What a situation; married four months, and they already have two children?

With Anna on his knee and watching the women

prepare the midday meal, Nicholas settled her confusion when she asked. "Park was married to a wonderful man, but he was killed in action before Anna was born."

"Mommy says I look like my Matt daddy." Sarah reported importantly.

Her dad enveloped her in his strong arms, "Yes you do. You are very beautiful." He kissed her curls.

Relief stole into Kathy's face against her will. She was not much of a Christian, but she did not think it right to have children before marriage. It thrilled her to find out that was not the case with her brother. She released a hushed, "Oh."

Nicholas continued to explain. "Matt was a very special person, and he gave me the two sweetest girls in the world." The look of absolute bliss fell across his face.

Even though it seemed as if everything was on the level, Kathy reserved a fear that this man and woman would bring her dad more heartache and this dream was another hoax. After a period of proving their claim was true, she allowed him and his family into the deepness of her heart.

By the time she returned to her newly built home a few weeks later, the long lost brother and his family had completely enamored Kathy. If only Mother and John were here to see this.

It was time that the O'Ryan family headed south, to resume their normal duties. Park and Nicholas begged the new Dad to come and stay with them for a while. Nicholas had just found him and did not want to lose him so soon. He wanted to take care of him for the rest of his life.

After finding out from Bob what Park had done for her family, Kathy felt she was hardly in any position to disagree. Besides, her father jumped at the opportunity. His stolen son wanted to take care of him, and he intended to see it happen.

However, Albert McCrain was not too fond of his son's wife being gone all the time for work. He was an old-fashioned man, who believed a woman should be home with her children.

Nicholas explained to him that keeping Park from what she loved best was like removing the wings from a bird, and he loved her for the position she took. 'Pop', as Park so lovingly called him, had no choice but to accept the circumstances.

They apprised Bruce and Christy of the latest happenings. They fell into an immediate liking of Albert McCrain. They saw a patriarch who would look over Park when Nicholas was not there.

Sonya and Sarah still insisted on spending as much time together as possible, but Sarah had a bond growing with Grandpa. He would take Matt and the girls out for ice cream, when all the moms and dads were gone to work. To his utter joy, he instantly inherited four new grandbabies. The heavens could not contain the thrill in his heart.

Kathy and Bob invited the girls to spend their summer vacation in Kansas with them, so Albert took them out the first two weeks in August.

Baby Talk

Dark circles formed around Mrs. O'Ryan's eyes, while sleep seemed to evade her restless nights, once more. She began a spell of nausea, which made Nicholas worry if she had lost that security she had with him. Perhaps, the past had reared its ugly head, and she was facing old ghosts, again.

She lost weight and began looking frail, as she threw herself harder into work to make time pass quicker. Everyone around her noticed the disheveled appearance.

Fred grabbed Nicholas, as he came in after debriefing one day, "Nick, I'm worried about Precious. She needs a doctor."

Nicholas retorted with a scoff, "It would be easier keeping a pig clean."

"I really think you should get her checked out."

The husband mused, "I might try to get her in to see Dr. Hart."

Fred frowned, "A shrink? Don't you think she needs a medical doctor?"

Nicholas had concerned himself over his bride, but had allowed her to reassure him she was fine. He shook his head. "I don't know. I wonder if it is not a mental thing."

Park was so sick of being sick that she volunteered to go before her husband could even suggest it. He accompanied her and held her hand tightly while the doctor spouted the normal doctoral jargon. He ran the standard tests and left them alone to await the results.

A little later, Dr. Kendall reentered the room with a grave expression on his elderly face. "The tests show that your condition will improve in eight months."

"Eight months?" asked Nicholas.

Park inhaled in disbelief, "Pregnant? I didn't think about morning sickness. I never imagined we could be pregnant."

"Fifteen weeks to be exact. Now if I could just ask your husband to step out for a few minutes, we will finish up here." The doctor gently suggested.

Park watched her husband leap from the room excitedly and then queried, "Why did my husband have to leave?"

Dr. Kendall turned back to the patient after the door closed. "What have you been doing to yourself?"

"Nothing unusual," she said innocently.

"Your body is in terrible shape. Have you been feeding this baby at all?"

"I have been really sick with this one."

"I will give you something for the nausea. You need to feed this baby. You had Anna natural, right?"

Park turned, "Yes sir."

"Quite honestly, I do not know if your body can handle another pregnancy. At your last physical, there were scars from years of abuse. I know you are a strong person, but I can't predict whether you can

359

carry to term or not. I strongly recommend doing a cleaning of the womb, before the baby has time to develop and endanger your life. You just are not strong enough."

Park's jaw hardened. This doctor was a long time friend that had delivered Sarah. How could he suggest an abortion? She stood appalled, "With all due respect, Doctor, no."

Dr. Kendall grumpily called Nicholas back in to retrieve his wife. "Mr. O'Ryan, your wife and baby are undernourished. It is imperative that she eats healthy from this point on, or she will not be able to carry this baby at all."

Nicholas's eyes fell upon his sweet love. She looked so discouraged. He would make it his mission to make her eat and regain her strength. He would employ Bruce, Christy, and even Fred into his service. Fred could stay on her at work and Bruce at home.

The regime worked. By the next doctor's visit a couple months later, Park gained eight pounds. The morning sickness had passed, giving her the benefit of nutrition, and her color was slowly reclaiming victory. Richardson put her on leave at the beginning of the sixth month, which assisted in her getting rest.

Park and the girls stayed at the Clayton home many times, while Nicholas was out on assignment, which enabled them to renew a friendship so dear. Bruce had been her tower of strength many times throughout her life. It seemed that lately they had drifted apart, with both having new marriages and families.

Nicholas went to the doctor visits with Park, each time getting more anxious than the time before. The day they did the ultrasound, he grinned at the monitor, when the OBGYN, Dr. Eaton announced that it was a boy. He heard the quick motions of the heart beating. His eyes spoke volumes to the only one who could read them.

For seven months, they waited ecstatically for the arrival of their precious little gift. Nicholas spent all of his free time fixing up the nursery. After finding out it was a boy, he repainted in blue and green and began purchasing décor that would be fitting for his little boy.

He couldn't have been happier. He never imagined that he would have so many blessings in his life. He rejoiced in God's goodness to him.

Sarah, Anna, and Pop had gone to Kansas to visit, but had plans to return in plenty of time for the birth. The girls excitedly argued over names for their new little brother. Everyone was preparing for the arrival.

Losing Faith

Park smiled to match her husband's smile. He kissed her knuckles, as he held her hand in his while watching the ultrasound. As soon as the monitor screen displayed the picture of their boy, they both turned their eyes to it.

Dr. Eaton was not normally a cheerful man, but his mouth formed a grimmer line than usual. His brow furrowed briefly, and he threw a quick glance at Park. "Excuse me. I would like to bring Dr. Kendall in for consultation. I'll be right back."

Neither husband nor wife wanted to voice that there could be a problem, but why else did he need consultation? Both tried to smile as if these thoughts were not racing through their minds.

Dr. Eaton and Dr. Kendall came in and looked at the silent monitor, while Dr. Eaton moved the wand over Park's belly. Nicholas looked at the doctors, but he was afraid to look at his wife. He was not sure what was going on.

Park realized that they were not hearing the heartbeat. She was afraid to look at her husband. She didn't need the doctor to tell her what was happening. His little heartbeat had stopped. She cried inside. She thought she had felt him kick this morning, but maybe she had been wrong. His heart was not beating. She had to let that sink in. Her precious little baby boy was in the presence of the almighty God. One lone tear escaped down the side of her temple.

Dr. Eaton shook his head sadly before leaving the room, and then Dr. Kendall lectured, "Park, you knew the risks from the beginning. I explained the odds to you. I am sorry, but your body just could not handle it."

She had not been strong enough. She had failed Nick in the thing he wanted most. She was so ashamed.

"What risks, Doctor? She has had two healthy pregnancies. Why is this time any different?"

"You were younger and stronger when Sarah was born. That pregnancy was traumatic on your reproductive system. Then, when you became pregnant with Anna, I warned Matt of the improbability of carrying to term. I told him that if you were physically able to have the second one, that it should be your last. It is a miracle that you even had Anna."

Park raised into a sitting position. "Dr. Kendall, why should a simple pregnancy be traumatic on my reproductive system?"

"The abortion you had destroyed your womb. You should never have let that butcher near you.'"

Nicholas turned to his ashen-faced wife and searched her eyes for the answer, only to find a blank. She sputtered, "I never had...an abortion!"

"The scars do not lie. I am telling you what I know the facts to be. We should do a DNC after the baby passes through your system."

Park no longer took heed to his words. She didn't understand. "God, you know my heart, you know it is not true. Please, help Nick to know it's not true either," she pleaded.

Nicholas deposited her at home without saying a word. She was glad for the silence. Park saw the pain and anger she had caused him. It was more than she could bear. She failed as his wife, just as she failed Matt and Lisa.

The husband mumbled something about going to work and left on his motorcycle, leaving his devastated wife in her guilt.

Park had never been one to stay where she was not wanted, and the look on her husband's face and his hasty retreat expressed clearly that he did not want her there. She threw her head up proudly. She would spare him the disgrace of leaving.

She took flight to her place of healing, but she feared Nicholas would search for her out of a sense of responsibility, so she gathered the appropriate camping gear and hiked two and a half days journey into the isolated woods.

She pitched camp near the foot of a bountiful

waterfall pouring diligently into its basin. The weather had cooled down this time of the year, but the days were still tolerable. During the warmest part of the day, she would submerge into the river to bathe and use the falling water as a means of relaxation.

For food, she hunted small game, and thus she began a hibernation of the desolate and condemned, praying constantly, "Oh God, forgive me. Help Nick to forgive me, also, according to Thy will, oh Lord."

Searching for Answers

Nicholas left Park without knowing any comforting words to help his beloved through this trial. He wanted to comfort her, yet nothing seemed appropriate. He left her to rest while he set out to prove his trust in his wife.

She was innocent of this accusation, and he would find the responsible party, so he diligently rode to the base in search of the one person who knew all about Park.

He included Bruce in on the doctor's visit in short time. "I am so sorry about the baby. How is Park?"

"She has not said anything about it. I left her at home to rest." Nicholas fidgeted with his fingers, and told him about the doctor's accusations.

Bruce shook his head. "I didn't know anything like that ever happened. Park would never go for anything like that." He pondered, "It had to happen before I met her. Really? It is hard to believe, but I wouldn't put anything past them. They are evil people."

With a tightened jaw, Nicholas questioned, "Them?"

Bruce nodded, "It is the only thing I can think of. She told me that she went to a Dr. B something one time. Let me think. It was Baker or Booker, or something like that. She could not recall why she felt so much animosity toward him, but she despised him. That was the only doctor she ever mentioned seeing."

"That is a start, anyway. I will look into that information. Thank you."

Bruce gave him a hearty handshake. "I am sorry, Brother. Christy and I will come over this evening, unless you would rather be alone."

"My wife would appreciate it."

The next line of business was to get the aid of Zoe to hack into ancient medical records from the probable hospitals where this could have taken place. She accommodated him with the doctor's name, Dr. Brooks, Ed Brooks.

Through his talent and means, he obtained the remaining information from the medical archives, which explained what he wanted to know. Now, he had proof of his wife's innocence and could present it to her to remove any guilt she was feeling.

That proved to be harder than he thought. After returning from his explorations in the mountains, he went home to comfort his bride, but she was not there. Had she gone to work? No, Richardson knew better than to call her in.

Late that night, he crawled into a sleepless bed without his mate, yet when morning dawned, she was still not there.

Richardson called early that morning to summon Nicholas to work. This did not sit well with him. He wanted to find Park. Upon asking, Richardson said he had not seen the missing woman in weeks. Where else could she be?

The assignment lasted four long days, and homecoming provided no further news of Park O'Ryan. Where could she be? He flew the small plane to their home in the mountains, but to no avail. He called Kevin in Montana, to inquire if she had been to the cabin, but he had not seen her there.

Another assignment claimed him. He distractedly performed his duty, all the while worrying about his absent wife. Too many things in this world could get her if he did not find her. More importantly than where was she, was why did she vanish? Had someone gotten to her? Had the evil found her?

"How is our father-to-be this afternoon?" Fred intruded into his thoughts, "Are you taking care of Precious and that baby Precious for me?"

Nicholas responded shortly, "She lost the baby, Fred."

Fred sobered, "Oh no! How is she handling it?"

"Truthfully, I do not know. I cannot seem to find where she has hidden herself."

"She's gone?" Fred asked in surprise.

"I have not seen her in twelve days." Nicholas was chomping at the bit to have this small talk over with so he could go in search of Park.

"Why didn't you say so sooner? It just so happens, I can help you in that matter."

Nicholas was half way out the door. He turned his head, "How?"

"Remember back when Park disappeared for a while?"

"Yes."

Fred grinned mischievously, "Well, I took it upon myself to keep track of her from that point on, so I planted a tracker on her thigh holster. As long as she wears it, we can find her."

Fred thought Nicholas was going to kiss him. Instead, "Fred, where is the transponder?"

"Over here, B549. According to this, she is in the northwestern part of the continent. Here is your exact longitude and latitude. Go find her and bring her back."

"Thanks, Brother, I owe you big," he called as he ran out the door, leaving Fred with a sigh of hope.

Nicholas contacted his father from the hangar who agreed to watch Sarah and Anna until he returned.

He did not share with him what was going on only that they needed some time alone.

The coordinates were not familiar to him, and he proceeded to the Montana area in which he knew they should be close. He reached the cabin to confirm this was not the right place. The compass told him to go north.

He hired a horse to carry him quickly to his distressed goddess. For the first time in his life, he was thankful that Park had made him ride those few times. After a full day's ride, he still did not have the right numbers.

How much farther could this be? His weary body ached from lack of rest. His head pounded with every hoof clomp. Aloud he cried, "God, please keep her safe in Your arms, until I get there."

The sun took cover hours ago. He could not think of anything, except finding the woman he held so dear. It was a matter of the horse directing him, rather than he directing the horse.

"North, northwest," screamed the silent compass.

Further still, they trod. It was six thirty the next morning, before he saw any sign of relief.

A dwindling fire yawned to go to sleep, with an occasional crackle making the only sound. Close by stood a tent by the edge of the clearing. At last, yes! The coordinates were close to perfect!

He sorely dismounted the mule ride and approached the tent with a noiseless step, but stopped dead in his tracks at the sound of a familiar clicking. He held his arms up and slowly turned around.

Finding Forgiveness

"Nicholas! What are you doing here?"

"Better question is why you are here?"

Park lowered and disengaged the shotgun, "I saw you needed some time to yourself."

"I needed time to myself? How did you figure that?"

"I am not blind." She turned so not to face him, "I couldn't bear being the one bringing you such torment."

"Park, you misunderstood."

"No, I didn't misunderstand anything. I could see how much you wanted this baby. I cannot give you the one thing you want most."

"We have Sarah and Anna, who are more than enough for me. I do not need other children. As long as I have you, I am happy."

"I tried to warn you, before you married me. You deserve someone untainted, who can give you all the things you so desire that I can't give you. I am soiled even more than I thought."

Nicholas followed her to the fire. "Listen to me. You were nine years old when this happened to you. You cannot hold yourself responsible for the things you had no control over?" he argued.

"It is *my* body. I should have control, no matter what the age. I was not strong enough for you. I could not make myself be what you need me to be."

"I have never met a more stubborn, hard-headed, uncompromising," he took her in his embrace, "yet enchanting woman in all my life. Where do you get these insane notions from?" The sun sparkled the golden strands through the mass of brown, while her face bore the innocence of a child.

She pulled away from his closeness, directing him a little way from the river. They stood before a small mound of rocks. Park sank to her knees, crying softly. "I buried little Albert Nicholas O'Ryan here."

He reached for her hand, "I am sorry I was not here for that difficult time. Honey, I want you to

376

understand. I was angry, but not at you. I knew that this news came as a shock to you. I will not lie, I am disappointed to lose our son, but that is only natural." He searched her blue eyes, finding little reprieve. "The reason I left was to find out what had happened to you so that I could comfort you."

"You did?"

"Yes, silly. You did no less for me in finding my family." He handed her a file.

She watched his fine movements, "You mean, you never thought that I..."

"Of course not. Honey, I have been going out of my mind with worry. I could not find you anywhere. You can't know what your disappearance has been like for me. You can never leave that way again, not without talking to me first, please."

Park did not seem convinced. "Nicholas, I will never bear you a blood child. Are you going to resent me for this?"

"Do you remember the vows I made to you at our wedding?" He recited, "I thank God for creating an angel for the sole purpose of becoming my wife. He predestinated before the beginning of time, that you should be the one that completed my life. I could not breathe, and you came bringing the air with you. I could not feel, and you brought me passion. Because of you, I have become a whole person, grounded in God, for God, and in the service of God. He is my eternal Refuge and Strength, and He gave you to me to be my helpmeet; and though mountains grow higher, and valleys grow wider, I will gladly give everything just to take this journey with you. Your beauty explodes to those around you, and all you touch turns gold. You are a balm for my pain, past and present. You are the one I love most next to God, and as long as He allows, I will make you proud of my love, safe in my arms, and cherished beyond your dreams. This is my vow to you, before God and these witnesses."

33587049R00213

Made in the USA
Charleston, SC
18 September 2014